Home Sweet Home, GOOD-BYE

Other Apple Paperbacks you will enjoy:

The Kissing Contest
by Dian Curtis Regan

The Hand-Me-Down Kid
by Francine Pascal

I Hate Your Guts, Ben Brooster
by Eth Clifford

Marrying Off Mom
by Martha Tolles

The Broccoli Tapes
by Jan Slepian

Home Sweet Home, GOOD-BYE

Cynthia Stowe

AN
APPLE
PAPERBACK

SCHOLASTIC INC.
New York Toronto London Auckland Sydney

Thanks to Nola Thacker,
editor at Scholastic,
for her patient, insightful, and supportive
editorial work.

ISBN 0-590-42759-8

12 11 10 9 8 7 6 5 4 3 2 1   3   1 2 3 4 5 6/9

Printed in the U.S.A.   40

To Peter Farrow

ONE

She told me that morning at breakfast while she was spreading orange marmalade on her English muffin. I should have known that something was wrong. Mom *hates* orange marmalade. I hate surprises.

She said, "I found this great place."

"Huh?" I was holding a spoonful of cereal two inches from my mouth.

"It's over on Elm."

"Mom, what are you talking about?"

"I've found our new house."

I dropped my spoon into the cereal. "We don't need a house. We've *got* a house."

"Charlie, you know we have to move."

"What do you mean, I know? I don't know." I got up from the table and stood, staring at her.

"We have to move."

"What? Since when?"

1

"You know about that agreement I signed with your father."

"Yeah, but my birthday was last year, and . . ." I walked over to the window and then back again, and then over to the sink.

"Your father didn't choose to sell then, but — "

"But what?" I wasn't exactly yelling, but it was close. Wandering around the kitchen didn't seem to be helping much, so I came back to the table and sat facing her.

Mom sighed. She started twirling her already curly long brown hair around her fingers. Mom's tall, and she looked taller still, sitting there completely erect. "We agreed that if he ever wanted to sell, he could."

"Who agreed?" I slammed my glass on the table and the orange juice splattered over what was left of both of our breakfasts. Mom just kept sitting there, half holding onto her coffee mug, half staring at me.

"Charlie," she said. "I'm sorry. I haven't known how to tell you. Your dad and Brenda want the money so they can get their own place. I've been checking around, and . . ." She was looking straight at me now. "I found a perfect home for us. We can afford it, and it's in a good neighborhood, and it's — " She stopped. She pressed her lips tightly together.

"But why didn't anybody say anything to me?"

"I should have."

"I thought that Dad was going to let us stay here until, until, I grew up or you got old, or something like that."

"It didn't work out that way," Mom said. "He wants to start a new life."

They'd gotten divorced when I was four. They'd owned the house together. They'd made this agreement that Mom and I could live in the house, rent free, until I was ten, and then they'd sell and split the profits.

I turned ten last year, and nobody did anything. Nobody even said anything, at least not to me. I figured they'd forgotten it.

Dad wasn't seeing Brenda then. Dad hadn't started seeing Brenda until last May.

"How come you didn't tell me then?" I asked.

"What do you mean?"

"When Dad didn't make us sell last year, I thought we could live here forever."

"Your dad didn't need the money last year. We talked about it, and we made a new agreement that we'd sell if he ever wanted to. But I didn't think, I guess I just didn't think that he'd ever want to sell."

"Looks like you were wrong."

"I know, Charlie. I'm sorry. I should have told you. I guess I never really thought we'd ever have to move." She started nibbling the corner of her English muffin, orange marmalade and all.

I sat at the table, staring at the designs my spilled

orange juice had made on our checkered table-cloth. Suddenly, I wasn't hungry. Losing your only home will do that to you.

"Charlie, it's just over on Elm, and it's a neat house. It's got a big backyard."

"I don't need a big backyard. I'm not a baby anymore."

"No, you're not." She was trying to tell me I was acting like one, but it didn't work.

"And Elm's in the Central district."

"Yes, it is."

"So, I'm going to have to change schools? Again? *Now?*" I'd just gotten to Jefferson Middle that September.

"Yes."

"And I won't be able to go to school with Mark anymore?"

"You can still be friends. You can ride your bike to his house."

"Big deal! What difference does it make if we can't go to the same school? We've always gone to the same school."

"I know."

"How come you couldn't find a place in this district?"

"I looked, Charlie, I looked. The places in this part of town have gotten too expensive."

"Great. So we're going to be living in a slum."

"No, it's not like that at all. It has a lovely porch that goes all around the first floor and it has a perfect room for my studio. And your room, you should see your room. It has this great ceiling that changes angles and I'll help you paint it whatever color you like and your posters will look terrific and . . ."

I stopped listening. I got up to go to school. Mom didn't seem to notice. She kept talking on and on about the genuine stained-glass window in the upstairs hallway, and it wasn't really a big place, smaller even than this house, but we were going to have plenty of room, and the ceiling in the living room was divine and the ceiling in the bathroom was wonderful. Suddenly, she was obsessed with ceilings.

I grabbed my jacket and started out the door.

"Charlie?"

"Yeah?"

"You're not too upset, are you? You're going to love the new place. I just know you're going to love it."

"Sure, Mom, sure." I was careful not to slam the door. I didn't want to slam the door. But I pulled it tight, fast, and when it was almost closed, I could feel the door shaking as I held onto the knob.

At first, I thought I'd broken the doorknob, because it felt stuck in my hand, but I looked down and saw that I was just gripping it tightly. I told my hand to let it go, and after a few moments, it listened to me. I headed on to school.

Two

As soon as I felt my fist in his stomach, I knew I was in trouble. He slugged me, hard, and I fell back. He kept hitting me, like he didn't notice that I wasn't fighting anymore.

I covered my face with my arms, but then I burrowed down and punched at his body with my fists. I kept punching at his stomach and then straightened up and pushed him against the wall. That's when he got me a good one in the face.

Mark grabbed me from behind, and then Sam was holding David. I felt something wet on my face.

"What's going on here?" It was Mr. Vincini. "I said, what's going on here?" He was coming up fast, almost running.

Nobody said anything. David had stopped trying to get away from Sam, and Mark had let me go. We all stood there, staring at each other.

"All right, I can see for myself. Charlie, have the

6

nurse check that nose and then report to my office. As for you, Mr. Ransome, just sit in the waiting room. I'll deal with you later."

It turned out my nose wasn't broken. I wasn't bleeding from my nose at all, but from where my braces had cut my lip. Mrs. Johnson had me rinse out my mouth. She patted my face with some cotton balls, and then she told me to leave.

"Don't you think I should lay down for a while?" I asked her.

"This injury was from a fight, right?" she asked.

"Ummmmmm," I said, trying not to move my jaw too much.

"Then it's your own darn fault," she said. "We don't coddle fighters around here. If you fight, you get hurt. Now get out."

Such a personality. I thought that sympathy was supposed to be part of a nurse's job.

I had to walk by David sitting in the waiting room of Mr. Vincini's office. It didn't look like I'd done any permanent damage, though he was still all red in the face. He was giving me looks that could kill.

"All right, Charles, what is this all about?" Mr. Vincini asked, as I sat on the edge of the big straight-backed chair in his office. I found myself staring at his balding head, fascinated by how the light seemed to jump off the top of his forehead, where hair should have been.

"I said, *what* is this all about?" he repeated.

"I called him a few names and he got mad, that's all, Mr. Vincini."

"What were some of the names you called him?"

"Like, a pimply faced jerk and a dead whale. I can't remember the rest."

Mr. Vincini's eyebrows went up. "What's he done to you?"

"Nothing."

"You pick on a kid twice your size because he's done nothing to you?"

"Well, uh — "

"You've never been in a fight before, have you? I've been checking your records."

"No, uh — "

"Then why'd you pick on David Ransome? You know, fighting's not allowed at this school. I hardly ever have to speak to a sixth-grader."

"I'm sorry, uh — "

"Plus, David Ransome's got a good fifty pounds on you. Are you two in some kind of trouble together?"

"No, uh, I just — "

"This doesn't make sense."

Mr. Vincini was right. It didn't make sense. David Ransome was six feet at least, and he had the body of a freight train. Everyone said that this was his third time in seventh grade, and everybody stayed away from him. If you walked by him in the caf you said, "Excuse me." Even the teachers left him alone. He looked mean.

8

"So let me get this straight," Mr. Vincini said to me. "For no particular reason, you decided today to call David Ransome names."

"Yeah."

"Any special reason?"

"No."

"You thinking about suicide or something?"

"No." How could I tell him that David's jacket had brushed mine when we were both getting our books from our lockers and that this had made me go nuts?

"I know you sixth-graders have adjustment problems but, Charles, physical violence is not allowed at this school. Is that understood?"

"Yes, sir."

"Well, all right. You've never gotten in trouble before. Detention for a week. And, Charles, stay out of trouble for the rest of the day. It's only first period."

By that point, I was worrying about staying alive for the day. From the look on David's face, sitting outside of Mr. Vincini's office, he still wanted to kill me. I made a quick exit by him, got a pass to History, and went to class.

At least there were only fifteen minutes left, one advantage to getting in trouble. I sat down next to Mark and tried to pretend I was fascinated by the discussion of the spread of disease during the Civil War.

Mark and I had been real lucky when we'd come

9

to Jefferson. We'd been afraid we'd be put in all different classes, but we were together for History and English, General Science and Typing. They had a special typing program for sixth-graders at Jefferson. Our lockers were in the same section, and we went to Phys. Ed. together. At Jefferson, the sixth-graders moved around just like the seventh- and eighth-graders, and having Mark in most of my classes helped a lot.

Not that it's going to help anymore, I thought, now that I have to move.

Of course Mark wanted to know all about what had happened. He stared at me, his thin face looking worried. While Mrs. Haldimand was writing excitedly on the board about smallpox and chicken pox and measles and influenza, he leaned over and whispered, "Are you nuts? You called him a *dead whale*."

"I know. I *know*."

"Why?"

"Don't bug me."

"But what's the matter with you?"

"Hey, man, don't bug me." Mrs. Haldimand had turned around and was staring at us. Fortunately, the bell rang just then, and I grabbed my books and got out of there without waiting for Mark. I went into the bathroom and stayed there a couple of minutes so I wouldn't meet him in the halls, and then I went to English.

Great, I thought. I'm here less than an hour, and

already I have the lurking hulk of the school out for my blood, and I'm hiding from my best friend.

Mr. Vincini didn't help things, either. I found out after English he'd suspended David for a week. If *I'd* gotten suspended and David had gotten detention, there might be some chance for my life. But now I knew that I was dead, absolutely dead.

Plus, deep down, I knew it wasn't fair. I'd started the fight. Just because I'd never gotten in trouble before and David wasn't so swift at schoolwork, he got suspended. It makes me wonder about the American system of justice.

THREE

I managed to stay out of trouble for an hour. All the kids made a wide berth around me. They knew that anyone crazy enough to pick a fight with David Ransome had to have something seriously wrong with them.

By third period, I actually started feeling better. I started thinking that my mother wouldn't really go through with it, that, sure, she'd found a house she liked, but she'd forget about it by that afternoon. My pleasant thoughts were rudely interrupted by Mr. Aberdinian.

"Do you care to join us, Charles?" he asked.

"Huh?"

Everybody laughed and I started feeling sweaty.

"Please start reading at the top of the page."

I shifted in my seat to buy some time.

"I said, start reading at the top of the page."

Harold Thompson angled his book away so that

I couldn't see the page we were on. Harold and I have never gotten along.

"What page is that, Mr. Aberdinian?" I asked. Everybody laughed. I don't know what was so funny about that. I hadn't meant to be funny, I was just asking a simple question.

"That's *it*," he yelled. "I've *had* it with you kids. Do you think I became a teacher so I could work with kids who don't know the page we're on?"

"But, Mr. Aberdinian — "

"Be *quiet*. I had to paint four houses last summer to pay my mortgage, and you can't keep your place. Out. Out! Report to Mr. Vincini."

"But, Mr. — "

"*Out!*"

I certainly couldn't report to the office. I figured Mr. Vincini would kill me if I showed up again so soon, so I went and hung around the boys' john for a while and then wandered into the back of the auditorium. The props room door was open, so I walked in there and sat down on the floor by the patch of light from the high little window. I started looking through my pockets to see if there was anything fascinating in there. There was nothing but my usual Swiss army knife and $3.32 and a dirty handkerchief. I'd always thought getting into trouble would be more exciting than this.

I tried to recite poetry, but that only took a minute because I only knew "One Snowy Evening." Mrs. Jetson had made me learn it last year for the stupid poetry recitation. Then I tried singing, but that could have attracted attention, so then I got creative. I counted all the costumes in the props room. Brilliant, huh? There were eight choir robes hanging up, four old-lady print dresses, three pink taffeta gowns, five army jackets, two little kids' fairy costumes (where did those come from?), eight skinny black skirts held onto hangers with safety pins, and this great Civil War costume, cardboard sword and all.

Then I got to the boxes on the floor. They were just filled with junk — piles of old dusty material, old shoes, a couple of Western boots in the middle of everything. Then I found the box full of old hats, hats like I've seen in pictures of the '20s.

There was a blue felt one with an ostrich feather and an enormous hat pin. I could see it all now. There's the beautiful damsel in distress being pestered by the vicious villain. He approaches her with dastardly thoughts in mind.

"Stay away," she cries. "Help, help!" The dastardly villain, thinking that here was a real find, approaches without caution. She calmly reaches up (he thinks to cover her gentle eyes), pulls out her hat pin, and — *whammo* — one less villain, gored to death.

You can probably tell that I was getting pretty bored. At the end of fourth, I figured it was probably okay to go to lunch. With all the real thugs in the school creating genuine havoc and chaos, I figured that Mr. Vincini wouldn't have the cops out for a person who'd been daydreaming in class.

I was wrong. I'd just gotten my limp spaghetti with the meatballs that looked slightly green, next to the canned string beans that looked slightly brown, and the definitely bright gold butterscotch pudding, when I saw Mark on the other side of the caf. I went to join him. He looked up and saw me and got this strange look on his face. I learned what the look meant as soon as I put my tray on the table, and felt this hand on my shoulder.

"Charles," said Mr. Vincini.

"Uh — "

"Now you've gone too far."

"I — I — "

"Mr. Aberdinian tells me you were disruptive in class."

"But, I — "

"Not paying attention."

"But, no, I — "

"And you were rude to him."

"No, I — "

"And then you chose to ignore his instructions to report to me."

"But, I — "

"That's enough. Get your things and go. You're suspended for a week. Come back with your mother next Monday morning to see me."

"But — "

"See you in a week."

He grabbed my tray and pointed toward the door. I looked back to see Mark turning green.

As I was slinking out of school a few minutes later, I decided to go and get a grinder at Fay's. Might as well enjoy my newfound freedom, right? Plus, I was starved. But as I got in front of the store, I glanced in to see David Ransome leaning against the counter, talking to Fay.

Maybe he's not such a bad kid, I thought. Maybe he's a real nice kid who just looks mean. Just because he's crummy at schoolwork doesn't mean he's a . . .

I paused at the door, almost pulling it open. Maybe he won't be so mad at me, now that I'm suspended, too. Here's my chance. I'll just tell him I'm sorry.

Then David turned slightly toward the door, and I took off. My mind said to talk to him, but my feet said to run. I listened to my feet. I ran. The gentle giant hypothesis was going to have to wait for another day.

FOUR

When I got to Dad's apartment later that day, Brenda was there, sitting at the kitchen table, writing a lesson plan. For her job, she teaches adults who can't read. Brenda says that there're a lot of them.

Brenda is pretty, I have to admit. She's completely different than Mom. Mom's hair is long and goes wild with curls. Brenda's hair is short. It's curly, too, but it's cut close around her head. Brenda's hair seems crisp, just like the rest of her. Even her movements seem crisp.

As usual, Brenda was wearing "an outfit." She had on a light blue silky blouse with a yellow scarf and a dark blue skirt. She never just wears a T-shirt and jeans, like Mom. She wears outfits. Everything matches.

Dad says that she doesn't make a lot of money, but she loves sales: garage sales, tag sales, store sales. Even Brenda calls herself a sales junkie.

I actually sort of like Brenda. That's part of the problem. I wish she was a real flake, or horrible and mean. Then I could hate her. But Brenda's kind of nice, and that makes me crazy, sometimes. It makes me so crazy because I don't know who to hate.

"Hey, Charlie, what's happening," she said, as she looked up and saw me at the door.

I stayed there. "Dad home yet?"

"He's buying dinner." Whenever Brenda was over, Dad got pizza. Brenda's a pizza fanatic. That's one of the things I sort of like about her.

"I'll wait outside."

"How was school?"

"Okay."

"Hey, you know what I heard today?"

I was already turning to go.

"Charlie, what's the matter?"

I slammed the door and was down the steps as fast as I could go. I thought about going home or going over to Mark's, but just as I was heading down the driveway, Dad drove in. He had on his Greek fisherman's cap, the one he always wears when he's in a good mood.

"Hey, sport," he said. "What's the rush?"

"Hi, Dad."

"I got your favorite, pepperoni and mushroom."

"Great."

"You don't look too enthusiastic."

"Yeah, sure. Hey, Dad, I don't feel too great. I'm going home."

"What's the matter, you sick or something?"

"Yeah, probably."

"Well, do you have a stomachache?"

"I just don't feel good."

"Do you have a fever?"

"I don't know. Probably. Look, Dad, I just don't feel good, that's all. I'm going home."

"Well, c'mon in, and I'll take your temperature."

"No, Dad. I want to go home."

"This is your home, too. You know this is your home, just like your — "

"Yeah, just like the one you're making us leave." I said it under my breath, but he heard me. He got this funny look on his face, and he started coming toward me, balancing the pizza in his left hand.

"Your mother told you? I wanted to tell you myself. I was going to tell you tonight."

"What's the difference? I still gotta move." I was shouting at him by then.

"Charlie," he said, holding me there by my arm. "I really need the money from the house. Brenda and I want to start a new life. We want to get our own place."

"And so you're taking ours away."

"It's not like that."

"So, what's it like?"

We stood there, staring at each other.

19

"Your mother and I, we've both lived too much in the past. Before I started seeing Brenda, well, you know how it was. Your mother and I were divorced, but we were still seeing each other all the time. I was always over there it seemed."

"I liked that. I liked you being home."

"But, Charlie, it's not *normal*. Your mother and I are divorced, we've been divorced for seven years. We've been acting like we're still best friends."

"Maybe you are."

"It's not that simple. It's not normal. We're divorced. We've got to start living our own lives."

I stood, staring at him. His fisherman's cap had twisted around so that the brim was over his ear. All of a sudden he grabbed me and pulled me close, and I was crying, sobbing into his jacket.

"It's okay, Charlie. The last thing I want to do is hurt you." He kept holding me, and I kept crying.

We'd both forgotten about the pizza. It was sliding out of Dad's hand. He tried to grab it, but it took an extra leap and landed on the driveway, upside down.

"Dead pizza," Dad said, handing me a handkerchief. I blew my nose about eighteen times.

"I tell you what, let's just go get a new one," Dad said. "You and me."

I didn't argue. And while we were waiting for the pizza, I told him about my fight with David Ransome and getting kicked out of school. Dad didn't yell. He just kind of laughed and told me that when he was my age, he'd been picked on since fifth grade by this kid named Bruce Hammerill. One day Bruce called Dad's mother a name, and Dad got fed up and belted him good. He flattened Bruce. He said that other than a lecture from the principal, he didn't even get in trouble. Dad said he got the distinct impression that his teachers were glad that he'd belted Bruce. The school didn't even tell his parents.

I asked him if he'd let me take karate, and he said maybe.

"Hey, Dad."

"Yeah?"

"Will you tell Mom?"

"About what?"

"About me being kicked out of school."

"You haven't told her yet?"

"Well, it was my night to come over here, and — "

"But you got kicked out at noon."

"Twelve thirty-five. I saw the clock in the caf as I left."

"What did you do all afternoon?"

"Hang around."

He was silent.

"So, will you tell her?"

"You should do it. It's part of being a responsible person, standing up and admitting what you've done."

"She'll take it better, coming from you."

"Well, I don't know."

"Please, Dad?" I gave him my best I'm-really-very-brave-and-mature-but-I've-had-a-hard-day-and-this-one-little-thing-that-you-could-do-for-me-would-help-me-so-much look.

The expression on his face didn't change, but I could tell he was giving in because his nostrils started dilating. It's kind of gross, but it's real helpful to know where he's at sometimes.

"All right, Charlie, just this once." I was right. I knew it. His nostrils never lie. He was continuing. "But I hope this doesn't mean that you're becoming a juvenile delinquent."

"Me? Are you kidding? I wouldn't have the guts."

FIVE

When we got back to the apartment, Brenda was already watching the news on TV. She'd left her papers spread all over the kitchen table.

"Hey, where's my pizza?" she greeted us. "It took forever!"

"We had a little problem," Dad said, winking at me.

"Well, Nat," she said to him, jumping up and kissing him on the cheek. "I never said I loved you for your punctuality." She laughed. "I just love you for being so sweet." She was tousling his hair. It was rather disgusting.

Brenda always has to jump up to kiss Dad because he's so tall. She's shorter than me, and he's six two. I wonder if I'm going to be tall? Right now, I'm pretty average, maybe on the tall side, but both Mom and Dad are tall, so I probably will be, too.

I went to get the plates and napkins. "Hey, grab

me a Coke, will you, Charlie?'' Brenda called.

''Sure,'' I yelled back. ''Anything else you want?''

''No, darling, just your wonderful company.''

Oh, sick, I thought, as I put her Coke in a glass. Why couldn't she just have said no thanks, like a normal person?

Then I saw it. I hesitated for a moment but then quickly bent down and picked up a little dead ant that was lying next to one of Brenda's papers that had fallen on the floor. I stood there, staring at it.

It's not her fault she's in love with my Dad, I said to myself. It's not like she's a home wrecker. Dad had been divorced for years when they met.

Yeah, I continued. (I was having a terrific conversation with myself.) But if Dad hadn't of met her, things would have stayed the same. He'd still be over all the time, and we wouldn't have to move.

That last thought did it. I put the ant in Brenda's glass. The foam oozed around it.

I almost threw the Coke out and got her another one. When Mark had told me last year about how he'd put salt in the sugar bowl on April Fools' Day, I'd told him how stupid and immature it was to do such a dumb thing.

He said that he'd sat there and watched Valerie, his sister, put two heaping spoonfuls on her cereal. On purpose, he told her that she shouldn't use so much, because sugar wasn't good for her. He knew that would make her put on another spoonful, because she hated it when he told her what to do.

He sat there and watched as Valerie raised the spoon to her mouth. She closed her lips around it and then her face froze. She spit it out, she stared at Mark, and then she screeched. She screeched the loudest screech Mark had ever heard.

Fortunately, he's fast, so Valerie didn't catch up to him right away. He did get a thirty-minute lecture from his mom, though, and he was grounded for a week. We both agreed that it had been worth it.

But putting a dead ant in Brenda's glass was a dumb thing to do, and I was heading toward the sink to pour out the Coke when I once again heard her from the living room.

"Hurry up, sweetheart, there's a cute little polar bear on the news."

"Don't call me sweetheart!" I said from between my tightly gritted teeth, as I stopped myself from throwing out the ant-laden Coke. "And why does she think I like cutesy little polar bears? She treats me like a baby!"

I entered the living room. Maybe she won't even find it, I thought, as I handed the glass to her politely. I knew it wouldn't hurt her because I'd had a science teacher in fifth grade who ate chocolate-covered ants, and I've swallowed loads of bugs that have flown into my mouth while I'm bike riding.

"Oh, thank you, darling," she said.

I sat and watched her.

"Hey, no appetite, sport?" Dad was watching me.

I grabbed a piece of pizza and stuffed it into my mouth.

"Hey, what's this?"

"Shh," Dad said. The polar bear was gone, and he was trying to hear some lady talking about crime prevention.

"Hey, look at this," she repeated.

"What's the matter, dear?" Dad asked.

"Look, there's . . . there's . . . a bug in my Coke."

"Oh, no! Let me see." He slid down on the couch next to her. "Oh, dear, it's a little — "

"It's a *BUG. A BUG.* IT'S A BUG."

"Calm down, Brenda, it's just a little bug. It looks like an ant, actually."

"How can they do this?" Her voice was high-pitched. "How can they sell such . . . such — ?"

I chimed in. "You know how they say there're tons of insects and rat droppings in candy bars and all that. The Feds allow it. They allow so many milligrams." I was talking faster than normal. They looked at me, and I realized that I should have just kept my mouth shut.

"Here, let me get you another Coke, Brenda," Dad was saying.

"Oh, I can't, I don't want one." She was looking at me strangely.

"It was just a little bug," Dad said. "C'mon,

Brenda, let's just forget about it." Dad was getting his let's-stop-this-foolishness tone of voice.

He brought her some orange juice. It was quiet, very quiet. I kept chomping on pizza, and Brenda kept looking at me, not quite staring, but almost.

"Well, didn't you see it?" she asked me.

"Whaddaya mean?"

"Didn't you see it — the *bug?*"

"Gosh, no, Brenda. I mean, it's all brown, the Coke and all. I mean, if it had been a Sprite . . ." I was still talking too fast and my forehead had started itching like crazy. I nibbled on a pepperoni.

"Why're you talking so fast? You feeling guilty or something?"

"Huh?"

"What do you mean, Brenda?" Dad asked.

Brenda didn't answer. She just kept looking at me.

"Well, if you mean something, say it," he continued.

Still watching me, Brenda said, "It just seems funny to me that Charlie didn't see that bug when he poured my Coke, that's all."

"It was a small little bug, not a big deal. We probably eat hundreds of them without knowing it," Dad said. He got off the couch and went and sat in the recliner, facing Brenda.

"You wouldn't have thought it was so small if it had been in your glass!"

"Hey, I'm sorry, I didn't see it," I said, holding

my head down. "I didn't realize I was supposed to be on bug patrol."

"Cool it, Brenda, he's only a boy."

"Yeah, a boy who needs to learn not to do cruel things. Right, Charles?"

"He's had a hard day. Lay off him."

"Lay off him? What about me? What have I done to deserve this? Is it my fault he's had a hard day? Is any of this my fault? You're the one who asked me to marry you. I told you that it wouldn't be easy, that we should wait."

"Brenda, I don't want to discuss this in front of Charlie." He was speaking very slowly but distinctly. He was holding onto the sides of the recliner, and his knuckles were white.

Brenda got quiet. She sat holding her glass and staring down at the floor. I'd finished my slice of pizza, but it didn't seem right to grab another piece just then.

We sat there for a long time, not saying anything. Half the pizza was still in the box and nobody was going for more. Then Brenda got up and walked into the bedroom and I thought I heard her crying. After a couple of minutes, Dad went in after her.

I thought about Valerie and the cereal. Somehow, that had seemed a lot funnier than the bug incident.

I thought that maybe I should apologize, own up to it. Maybe then, Brenda would stop crying.

I was halfway to the bedroom door, but I could

hear them talking and I figured I'd apologize later. Maybe.

I felt awful. I didn't think that things could get worse than having a bad fight and getting kicked out of school, but they had. And this time, it had been my fault. It had really been all my fault. I couldn't do anything right.

And then I remembered that there still could be trauma to come: Mom didn't know yet about my suspension. With that pleasant thought, I folded the pizza box shut and put it in the refrigerator. Somehow, I wasn't hungry anymore.

Six

Lena called Tuesday afternoon. I told her what had happened, about us having to move because Dad was marrying Brenda.

"And I got kicked out of school."

"You what?"

"I got kicked out of school."

"Why? What did you do?"

"I had a fight with David Ransome, but really it happened because of Harold Thompson."

"Who's he?"

"He's this kid who hates me. He didn't let me see the page we were on in English."

"That doesn't seem so awful."

"It's a long story. I was having a bad day."

"But, Charlie, you never get in trouble. How long are you suspended for?"

"A week."

"What did your mother say?"

"Oh, she ranted a little, but she's not too mad. She feels guilty 'cause she thinks she shouldn't of told me about moving right before I went to school."

"You're lucky."

"I know."

"How big is this David kid?"

"Big, very big. Huge, like an elephant."

"Aren't you afraid he's going to kill you the next time he sees you?" she asked.

"The thought's crossed my mind once or twice," I admitted.

"Well, what are you going to do?"

"What can I do? I'll just try to blend in with the furniture. I'll put a piece of paper on my head and pretend I'm a school desk."

She laughed. "But, no, I mean really?"

"Really, Lena, I don't know."

We were both silent.

"So when are you going to move?" she asked lightly.

"Mom's just put the deposit down on the dump on Elm."

"Elm? You're moving to Elm?"

"Yeah."

"Oh." She was silent, strangely silent.

"What's the matter?" I asked.

"Your new house is over on Elm?"

"Yeah."

She didn't say anything, not a word. All of a sudden, I got it. I couldn't believe I hadn't thought of it before. Lena went to Central. If we moved to Elm, I'd be going to Central. Lena and I would be going to the same school!

It was a shocking thought. See, other than Mark, Lena was my best friend. We'd been friends since the summer, when her little sister Emily was playing with the telephone, and Emily was calling up people and playing a tape and telling them if they named that tune, they'd win a trip to Hawaii.

One day, Emily got me, and I knew exactly what she was doing because Mark and I used to do that when we were little twirps. I didn't have anything to do that afternoon, so I was stringing Emily along. All of a sudden Lena cut in. She'd caught Emily red-handed (or should I say, phone-handed?).

Lena apologized, and I said I didn't mind because I didn't really believe I was going to win a trip to Hawaii. We got to talking and we've been friends ever since. We've been good friends. We call each other almost every day, and I tell her things sometimes that I don't even tell Mark.

I've never been friends with a girl before. But I don't think of Lena as a *girl*. I just think of her as my friend.

Except that we've never met. We've just been friends on the phone.

Great, I thought. So now I'm going to have

to meet Lena. What if she's a dog? What if she thinks I'm a dog? *What if she's beautiful?* And how am I supposed to be good friends with a girl? I mean, a girl I have to be in school with all the time?

I sat there on the floor of our kitchen, like I always did. I started staring at the stove. Very interesting, I thought. Stoves are really most interesting. Chrome-and-white fronts and . . . oops, there's a spot, probably from the chili we had the other night. I actually started rubbing at the spot with the edge of my shirtsleeve.

All of a sudden, Lena was speaking. "Well, are you sure you have to move?"

"I've never seen Mom like this. She's bought curtains for the new place."

"Does she want to move?"

"I guess so, but I don't understand it. She's never said anything about it before. She always raves about this place, about how much she loves it."

"Well, maybe she'll change her mind."

"Well, maybe."

We were both quiet, but Lena had kindled a hope in me that maybe something would happen and we wouldn't have to move after all. Maybe Dad and Brenda would have a terrific fight. Maybe Mom would come to her senses and refuse to move. Maybe Brenda would decide that she wanted somebody richer than Dad and she'd dump him. *Maybe our house wouldn't sell.* That was a good one. That was a great one. That one could happen.

"Maybe our house won't sell," I told Lena.

"Yeah, that could happen. My mother knows these people that tried to sell their house for two years and nobody bought it."

"Really?"

"Yeah."

"That's great. I could be out of school, I could be working. I could be all grown up."

We were both quiet for a minute, and then Lena said, "Well, if you do come to Central, it'll be okay. I mean, it's a pretty big school, and maybe we won't even meet. We can still be friends."

"With our luck, we'll be in all the same classes."

"I know."

"But, like, we could pretend we don't know each other and just be friends after school."

"Do you think we could?"

"Sure. But I don't think I'd like that. It sounds like something Emily would do."

"Yeah. Oh, do you know what she did this morning?"

"What?"

"She hates her new teacher so she didn't want to go to school so she tried to pretend she was sick."

"The old thermometer-under-the-tap-water trick, huh?"

"Yeah, how did you know?"

"I've done it once or twice myself."

"But she messed up because she forgot to shake it down to a hundred and one or something sensible like that. When Mom read it, it was a hundred and six. She had a fit."

"Poor Emily. She's got to learn to be a better sneak. She always gets caught."

"I know, we should give her *sneak* lessons."

We both laughed at that, but then we had to get off the phone because Mom and Adelaide, Mom's best friend, got home just then. Mom's always bugging me about being on the phone too much. She's put me on a fifteen-minute schedule.

They'd been out all afternoon, talking to realtors.

"How do I choose?" Mom asked. "They all seem the same."

"The Schneider woman has a reputation of getting the job done," Adelaide answered. "Let her sell it." Adelaide wasn't one *not* to express her opinion. Adelaide was a definite person. She even looked definite. She had black hair, which she wore long and straight, very light skin, and hazel eyes that somehow I always noticed.

"I'm not sure I like her," Mom said. "She's too . . . too . . . short."

"Like Brenda?" I asked. The question came out of nowhere. Mom and Adelaide both gave me dirty looks.

Adelaide looked at her watch. "Oh, wow, I've got to rush, dear one," Adelaide said. " 'Bye, Charlie."

It was so weird, but as soon as she was out the door, a serious question just popped out of my mouth, out of nowhere.

"Hey, Mom," I asked her, as she was hanging up her jacket. "How come you and Dad never got back together again?"

"What a funny question to ask me now."

"I just wondered."

"We've always stayed good friends, but . . ."

"But what?"

"Well, you know, I'm a silversmith. I have my own business, and your dad sells life insurance."

"So what?"

"He's always on time. His idea of being daring is to order blue cheese rather than Italian for his salad dressing."

"C'mon, Mom, it's not that bad."

"I know, but I like to ride in hot air balloons."

"Remember when you tried to get me to do it?"

"I certainly do. Your father had a fit."

"I had a fit."

"Yeah, but that's what I mean."

"But that doesn't seem like such a big deal to me. You're always laughing when he's around."

She got quiet. "I know you miss him." She started rearranging the placemats on the dining room table. "I've got a lot of work to do. I've got to finish that necklace for Mrs. Smithurst."

"But, Mom — "

"Bring in the trash barrel, will you? And, Charlie?"

"Yeah?"

"Never mind."

Seven

Once I knew that Mom and Dad weren't mad at me, I thought I'd *like* being suspended. But I didn't. There wasn't anybody around to do anything with, and Mom nixed the idea of my watching TV during the day. Her studio is attached to our living room, and she refuses to listen to the television while she's working.

But she does watch *The Young and the Restless* while she has lunch. I was so bored, I actually watched it with her a couple of times.

Mark kept me posted on the big things during that suspension week, like Harold getting caught putting a rubber snake into Mr. Aberdinian's top desk drawer. It's so typical of him, but I was thrilled that this time he got caught!

I'd called Mark on Monday night and apologized for being so weird at school. He understood when I told him about my having to move.

He said, "You should have just told me."

"I couldn't. It felt like the words were stuffed in my mouth and couldn't come out."

Mark understood. Mark is like my brother, we've been friends for so long. Before I met him, I felt cheated that I didn't have a brother or a sister, but for the last few years, I haven't cared. I wonder if Dad and Brenda will have kids. If they do, I wonder if they'll be tall and thin like Dad, or short and compact like Brenda. Of course, they'd only be my half brother or sister, anyway.

It was Thursday afternoon, and we were hanging out in my room, listening to the Talking Heads. "Look at all this stuff," he said. "You're sure going to have to throw out some junk."

"Whaddaya mean, junk?" I answered. "Every single thing is a priceless memory of my lost childhood."

"Yeah, sure, like these old orange peels."

I laughed, and ducked as he threw one at me. I scooped it up and got him in the shoulder, as a handful more shot back at me.

"Hey, what a lousy shot."

"I got you four times and you know it."

"Riiiiiight. C'mon, let's go get a Coke."

When we got to Fay's, I was already in the door before I saw him, sitting in an end booth with his elbows on the counter and his right leg propped up on a nearby chair. He started getting up when he saw me.

There was nobody else in the place. Fay must

have been somewhere out back. Mark stayed right with me, I'll give him credit for that. I felt a little better with Mark standing right next to me.

My feet seemed planted to the floor. David got up and started walking toward us, but he was walking real slow.

Without thinking, when he was just a few feet away from us, I said, "David, I'm sorry."

He stopped and looked at me. I thought I saw a look of surprise in his eyes, so I kept on. "I was in a real funk that day, and I'd gotten some bad news and I took it out on you. I'm sorry I got you in trouble."

He shrugged. Then he said, "Get out of here." There didn't seem to be any expression on his face. He just said simply, "Get out of here."

We did. We didn't wait around for any explanation. "How come he didn't belt you?" Mark asked.

"I have no idea." My heart was still making these loud, booming, panic-stricken noises in my chest.

"Maybe because it was at Fay's and he's friends with Fay?"

"Maybe, but it doesn't make sense. There was no one in the place, and he didn't kill me."

Mark and I walked around for a while. It seemed like the right thing to do. Once my heart had gone back to normal, I had all this energy, and I couldn't just sit around. So we walked. We walked down Elm Street and across Bridgeton and then up Wallace and over to Pleasant. Then we did the loop, again.

When I suggested a third loop, Mark said he had to go home. I couldn't blame him. I wasn't much fun to be with that afternoon. Not that I'm terrific company during normal times, but that afternoon, all I could think about was what torture David Ransome was planning for me. I was convinced that he hadn't beaten me up because sudden death was over too quickly. He wanted to make it slow.

I walked our loop a couple more times and then went home. The phone was ringing as I got in the door. It was Lena.

"You need a bodyguard," she said, after I blurted out what had happened.

"No kidding. And where am I going to get one?"

"That's my idea. I've invented a whole new business. It's called 'Rent-a-Thug.' "

"Right."

"I'm serious. The slogan could go like: 'Are you being picked on at school? Are you being tormented and harrassed?' "

" 'Are you a pimply faced wimp who's tired of running away from the big brawny brutes at your school?' "

" 'Call Rent-a-Thug.' "

We were both in hysterics by then. "And then there could be different models of thugs you could rent," she went on.

41

"Yeah," I said. "You could get the model chosen to just quietly intimidate."

"Or the one that would beat up anybody you didn't like."

"But where would we get our thugs from?"

"Football players in the off-season, ex-weight lifters, people like that."

"Okay, but how are you not going to get caught?"

"Oh — strict confidentiality is part of the system."

The more I thought about Lena's idea, the more I liked it. "Hey, we could totally change the way kids relate to each other."

"Yeah, you wouldn't have to be huge to not have people want to pick on you."

"It's not just that."

"I know, but having a thug would sure be great."

We both agreed on that.

Lena's mom wanted to use the phone then, so she had to get off. It had been great, though, just like old times. We hadn't mentioned me moving to Elm once.

The bell rang. It was the realtor Mom had hired, a Mrs. Schneider from L.R. Realty.

I opened the door for her, and even though she was my height, she looked right through me to start talking to Mom. Her lips kept moving in all these odd little shapes because she had on the thickest, reddest lipstick I'd ever seen anybody wear. She had a voice like Attila the Hun.

"Wonderful, wonderful," she said. "This place is wonderful. It's sure to sell fast. Houses in this neighborhood are selling like hotcakes. Wonderful, wonderful."

"Hello, Mrs. Schneider," I said in my polite voice.

"Oh, hello. Is this your darling boy? Oh, wonderful, wonderful, this place will bring a bundle."

I should have noticed it then, but I didn't. As she was showing Mrs. Schneider "the place," Mom kept saying things like, "Well, the toilet does leak in damp weather."

"Of course you know I'll need exclusive rights," Mrs. Schneider said.

"And it's rather cold in the winter because we have so few windows facing south."

"Wonderful, wonderful, oak cabinets, these old cabinets are wonderful." She was opening all our cabinets at random. What did she want to see? If we had something hidden in there?

"The floor's a little warped in the living room," Mom added helpfully.

"I love these closets. Buyers love lots of closet space." She was opening all our closets and looking in. I wasn't going to let her do that in my room.

"We have lots of trouble with ants in the summer," Mom said. To listen to her, you would have thought that she's hated living here all these years. Like I said, that should have clued me in to our future problem, but it didn't.

We finally got rid of Mrs. Schneider. Mom and I both went into the kitchen and I made her a cup of coffee and she made me a root beer float. Then we baked brownies and oatmeal cookies. My appetite was fine. I was going to start getting fat if things didn't settle down.

EIGHT

Mom and I got to school early Monday morning. I told her I wanted to wait until all the kids were in class, but she said she didn't want me missing any more school than was necessary. Great.

Mr. Vincini was polite. He kept saying things like, "Charlie's never been in trouble before. There was nothing on his record. I can't imagine what got into him."

Mom agreed, and then she complimented him on his tie, and then he said how his wife has a piece of her jewelry, and then Mom said, "Which one?" And he said, "The silver robin," and Mom said, "Oh, yes, that's always been a favorite of mine." And they went on and on and on.

After about fifteen minutes, they finally noticed me, and Mr. Vincini mumbled something about me not letting it happen again, and Mom said something about how of course it would never happen again, glowering at me all the time. I never had a chance to say a word.

I went to get my stuff from my locker. I was almost there when I saw David Ransome at the end of the hall. I considered having some pride and walking right up to him and saying, "Hey, old chap, you seem like a nice enough person. Why don't we bury the hatchet and just be friends?"

Then I reconsidered the cost of pride, and I figured that it would be nice to stay out of trouble — not to mention the hospital — for the morning. So, once again, I slunk into the nearest doorway and waited until he was gone. The funny thing is, I think he saw me. For all of his crummy reputation, David hadn't gone after me yet, and he'd had a couple of chances.

The morning was boring. I thought I'd get a big reception back, like maybe there'd be a banner over my homeroom door, saying, "Welcome Back, Suspendee." But nobody seemed to notice that I'd been away for a week.

I stayed cool. I kept out of trouble. I'd even done my homework when I was out for the week. Mark had brought it over every afternoon, and I'd done it in the morning. This wasn't from virtue, it was from boredom.

That week I'd been suspended I'd read through my entire *Far Side* collection four times. I'd fixed a Porsche model I'd messed up in fourth grade. I'd gone through every penny in Mom's penny jar, looking for rare coins. I didn't find any, just a lot of '65s and '72s.

That week I'd found myself *liking The Young and the Restless*. It was very depressing.

I'd gotten out the 1,000-piece hamburger puzzle Dad had given me for my birthday. I still couldn't do it.

Mom had suggested that I clean up my room. *I'd actually considered doing it for ten minutes or so.*

That week I'd discovered there really was something I hated more than schoolwork, and that was doing nothing.

So I settled back into school. The most exciting thing that happened all day was the note I got from Mark in typing class. It said,

"dear   charlie, YOu are very ugly and stupid"

Naturally, I had to respond. "dear MARK, I may be ugly and stupid, bbut at least I can type better than you can."

"Your feet smell xxxxx like day old manure."

"Your ears look like PArachutes."

"Your nose is   so big an army could camp in one nostril"

"you don't need breath mints, xxxxx you need breatth wafers!"

Then he wrote, "maybe you should meet lena."

"what if she has xxxx zits all over her nose/?"

"It'd be better to xx find out now. Besides, you've got zits on your nose"

"Only a couple, and they're temmporary. But

47

what if she'ss got scraggly hair and xxxx buck teeth and wears glasses?"

"What if she's blond and GORGEOUS?"

"Even worse!!!!"

"you could meet at the mall . ."

"Yuck."

"Chicken."

"Squawk, squawk, squawk."

"i mean, you don't have to spend xxxx the whole day. you could xxxxxxxx just meet her there for a little while, and then if you hate her, you can take off"

Mrs. Ostowsky wandered by just then, so we had to cool it. Mrs. Ostowsky isn't all that swift. Most of the time she just reads magazines at her desk once she's given us our assignment, but she's not totally gone. Mark and I started typing rows of letters like mad.

I thought a lot about what Mark had said, though, and that afternoon when I got home, I gave Lena a call.

After I told her about Mark's idea, she was quiet for a few moments, but then she said, "After all, we are in sixth grade. We've got to be mature about this. And I can walk to the mall."

"I can get a bus," I told her. "Let's meet in front of the fountain about three-thirty."

"Okay, uh . . ."

"Yeah?"

"How will I know you?"

"Well, uh, I'll wear my bright blue Jefferson jacket."

"Okay. And, um . . . how tall are you?"

My heart sank. At that moment, I knew she was a giant and was hoping I was huge. "Tall, pretty tall, I'm five six," I lied. I'm really five five.

"Oh, and, um . . ."

"How tall are you?"

"Oh, I don't know, about the same, five five or so."

"What color hair do you have?"

"Blonde."

"Blonde?" My heart sank. She *was* going to be gorgeous.

"Well, it's got some brown in it. It's really kind of half blonde and half brown. In the summer it gets bleached by the sun."

I felt a little better. I figured she had dirty blonde hair. "I have brown hair," I told her.

"Oh."

"Well, uh, maybe we should send each other our picture so we'll know what we look like."

"Yeah, we could, but . . . there won't be time by tomorrow."

"Oh, yeah."

I knew that it had better be tomorrow, or I'd never do it.

"Well, see ya," she said.

"Yeah, see ya." The amazing thing was that to-morrow we would.

NINE

That next afternoon, Mark and I stopped back at my house to change before going to the mall. I wore my Prezzia rugby shirt, the real one with the rubber buttons that Dad got me last year, and my good jeans and Adidas sneakers.

"Maybe I shouldn't wear my best jeans," I told Mark. "She'll think I'm stuck-up." I started pulling my old pair out of the drawer.

"Yeah, but those have holes in the knees. She'll think you're a slob."

We settled on the rugby shirt and the good jeans. Mark had on his blue sweater and cords, but that didn't matter because he was only going to come with me and wait until we saw her and then take off.

The bus let us out in front of the J.C. Penney entrance. I started walking slowly.

"C'mon, hurry up. How bad can this be?" he

asked, as he grabbed my arm and started pulling me along.

"I think I left something on the bus."

"Yeah, sure, like your brain."

"C'mon, Mark, I don't think this is such a good idea."

"What've you got to lose? If she's weird, you say, 'Hi, nice meeting you,' and then you take off quick and never call her again, that's all."

"What if she thinks I'm weird?"

"Then she's smart! C'mon." He really grabbed me this time as I was starting to turn back toward the bus stop. "Stop being such a chicken."

I stopped. He was right. I took a deep breath, did a 180, and started walking toward my fate.

The mall was quiet, with only a few people wandering around. The ladies fashion stores were open, offering thousands of shirts and slacks and dresses. The background music changed as we walked by each one, calling out that in *this* store, teachers could buy clothes, and in *this* store, teens would be happy.

I found myself fascinated by all the objects for sale. I almost wanted to go into the Pine Furniture Factory. Mark kept pulling me along.

"Hold it," I said to him, as I grabbed his arm and pulled him into The Limited.

"What's the matter?"

"That's her. I know that's her." I was pointing toward a girl who was fondling some jeans on a rack. Her bright yellow hair matched her tight, two-belted pants perfectly. As she turned around, I saw the cigarette dangling from her mouth.

"Hey, I thought you weren't supposed to smoke in here," Mark said.

"She's not smoking it, it's not lighted," I told him, trying to hide behind a rack of sale dresses.

The girl — Lena, I was sure — turned toward us and started coming over. I didn't know whether to run or do a nose dive on the floor, but in my confusion, I turned around fast and bumped into a jewelry display case.

"Whaddaya kids want, anyway?" the Lena girl said, as she took the "cigarette" out of her mouth. It was really some kind of marking pen.

"I, uh — "

"I hope you ain't come to lift anything."

"Oh, no, nothing like that."

"You work here?" Mark asked.

"Yeah, you want something?"

"Well, I — I was going to get something for my sister for her birthday."

"Well, look around, but I'll be watching you." She started marking some tags with her pen, and I could see her watching us the whole time we were in the store. I'd never really looked at clothes in a women's store before, and I was surprised at how they all looked the same that day, all pastel colors and all about the same size.

"Did you see her hair?" Mark gasped, as we

finally got out. "It was dyed that color."

"I know, I know. C'mon, we better hurry up."

There were a few people standing around the fountain as we got up close. There were two old people sitting on the bench, holding hands and talking. There was a woman with a baby who was bawling, and a couple of high school kids with punk haircuts.

Mark ducked into Miller's Drugs, like we'd planned, and I walked toward the fountain, hoping to look cool and relaxed. I started thinking that maybe she wouldn't show, but then, there she was, right in front of me.

She wasn't six feet tall and she didn't wear weird glasses, and she didn't have on a ton of makeup or tight, two-belted jeans, and she wasn't wearing blue socks with red sneakers or a polka-dotted shirt with a yellow-and-black miniskirt. And she wasn't beautiful. She was a girl I probably wouldn't have noticed at school.

"Hi," she said. "Charlie?"

"Yeah, hi," I said. "Lena?" Boy, this was going to be a terrific conversation. "Did you have trouble finding the place?"

"No, I come here all the time."

"Oh." My ears were starting to itch, but I kept my hands down. Ignore them, I thought. And think of something intelligent to say. My ears kept itching, and then my nose started to feel strange. My mind was filling with more pleasant thoughts.

Great, now I've got some contagious rash that's going to spread all over my body. Maybe it's leprosy, maybe it's —

"You come here a lot?" Lena was asking.

"Yeah. Mark and I come here on weekends and hang out." All of a sudden, I had to sneeze, and then I realized that my handkerchief was in my other jeans. I tried to stop it, but I couldn't, and Lena saw in one second what a slob I really am. At least I didn't sneeze all over her — I just sneezed all over my shirt sleeve.

"Here, I've got a Kleenex in my purse," she said. As she started to open it, somehow the clasp burst open, and all the stuff in her purse fell out on the floor. There was a wallet and an eyeglass case and a comb and a couple of papers and some other stuff I didn't see too well, because she was down on her hands and knees grabbing everything.

"Here, I can help," I said, bending down.

"No, no, I can get it." It seemed like she didn't want me to help. She was fast. In a flash, she had everything back in her purse and she was standing up again. She laughed a little, but it didn't sound at all like her telephone laugh. "Here, here's a Kleenex."

I grabbed it. I'd forgotten that I had the remains of a sneeze on my face.

As we stood there, staring but not looking at each other, I noticed that she was wearing a pink polo shirt and Guess? jeans. She had on little star earrings that kept catching the light of the fountain. Her hair was short and curly, and I could see why she had trouble describing the color to me. It was mostly blonde, but there was some brown in it. Her hair was nice.

All of a sudden, she was speaking. "So, what do you want to do?"

"I don't know, you want to walk around?"

"Yeah, okay."

We passed Mark, still in Miller's Drugs. He looked up as we passed, but I ignored him. I'd tell him about it later, like we'd agreed.

Lena and I walked around the first level, and then the second, and then we got Cokes at Friendly's. She told me that her cat had had kittens that morning, and her parents were going to let her keep just one. Did I want a kitten? I told her I didn't know. Then we were quiet, and then we talked about the weird-looking shoes in Rosten's window. I told her about seeing this woman wearing high-heeled purple shoes with red bows and jingles. She laughed about that. It was almost her telephone laugh.

We walked around for a little while after Friendly's. A couple of times I forgot we were together in person, and I talked to her like I do on the phone. But most of the time, I just felt like staring at her from the corner of my eye, and I didn't really know what to say. Everything I said sounded stupid.

Finally, it was time to catch my bus.

"Well, uh, it was nice meeting you," I told her.

"Me, too," she said. She seemed sincere.

"Well, uh, break a leg." As soon as I said it, I was sorry. "I mean, like, don't *really* break a leg."

She saved me. She laughed. "Oh, I know," she said. "You mean like in the theater when actors tell each other to break a leg for good luck."

"Yeah." Lena was really pretty nice. "Well, I'd better go. I'll see ya."

"Yeah, I'd like that," she said.

I didn't even notice the bus ride home. When I'd said "I'll see ya" to her, did that mean that I'd actually have to see her again? Did I want to see her again? Did I want to *not* see her again? Did she want to see me again? She *had* said that she'd like to, but maybe she was being polite. She couldn't exactly have said, "Actually, Charlie, I think you're just about the most boring person I've ever met, and seeing you again would be extremely depressing."

Maybe I shouldn't have said *anything* about seeing each other. Maybe I should have said something like, "Well, it was most pleasant meeting you, Lena. Good-bye." But that sounded all wrong, like something a grown-up would say.

Maybe I should have — I stopped myself. I was driving myself crazy. I walked over to Mark's and told him all about it. He said that he thought that she looked like she was having a nice time when he saw us walk by, but he only saw us for a couple of minutes so it was hard to tell.

Mark also said he thought it wasn't so bad that I'd said something about seeing her again, because people say that all the time when they don't mean it. But I did mean it, at least a little, but I'm not completely sure that I did.

Mark and I pooled our money and went down to Fortin's Drug and bought a half gallon of Double Mint Fudge ice cream. We finished it together, sitting on the curb in front. We both like eating right out of the box.

TEN

Our house sold in three weeks. "Isn't it amazing," Mom kept saying. "All that worry for nothing."

I hadn't worried it wouldn't sell. I had worried it would, but no one was asking for my opinion these days. The day of doom (the closing) was December the ninth.

From the minute we put it on the market, it was loaded with people, all kinds of people. We had a regular-looking couple with a teen-age daughter who had a mohawk, a college professor who studied fish physiology (he insisted on telling me all about it), a tiny woman with long blonde hair who seemed harmless enough until she got into our kitchen and started pulling all our things out of our cabinets.

By then, I was used to people opening all of our cabinets and closet drawers. I just wasn't used to people pulling things out. Mrs. Schneider handled

58

her well, I'll admit. While Mom stood there sputtering, and the woman kept yelling about wanting to find out the true story about how the cabinets were made, Mrs. Schneider just grabbed her arm and pulled her out of the kitchen. Mark and I were impressed. Mrs. Schneider could definitely make a terrific bouncer.

Throughout it all, Mom kept talking about how glad she was that we were getting so many people to look at the house. But she also kept telling all the people about the mice that run around the walls at night. I personally like them. I think of them as little friends, but I don't think other people want to hear about them, especially when they're thinking about buying our house. Mark thought that it was funny that Mom was telling people about the mice, too.

This couple with two bratty kids finally bought it. When I got home from school on Wednesday, there was a new Ford station wagon in our driveway, and the two bratty kids were running around outside. The larger one started climbing on the jungle gym Dad had put up for me when I was little.

"Hey, get off that," I yelled to him. He stuck out his tongue at me. I started walking over to give him the one-two, but just then Mom came out the front door with the couple. She was gushing and ooohing, saying things like, "Oh, I'm sure you're going to love the house," and then the next minute she was saying, "Of course, I'm sure you won't mind the Hendersons' dog. He only barks all night in the summer, but you can put on your air conditioner and that drowns out the noise."

Pulling at the couple, trying to get them out of Mom's grasp, Mrs. Schneider started running around the front yard, showing them the chrysanthemums and the hemlock trees and the juniper bushes.

"Things aren't growing too well lately," Mom was saying. "I don't know if it's some kind of pollution, or what, but I lost every single one of my tulip bulbs last spring."

The couple wasn't paying any attention to Mom. As soon as they got into our yard, they started yelling at their kids at the tops of their voices. The two brats didn't pay any attention to them.

Finally, Mrs. Schneider went over and grabbed the two kids and got the family in the car and sped away. Mom was yelling, "Don't worry about cooking on moving day — I'll bake you a casserole." What did she think she was going to be doing on their moving day?

Mom knew they were moving in, but she seemed a little confused about us having to move out.

I was starting to realize that I had more problems than just dealing with my own life falling apart. I was starting to realize that I was going to have to worry about my mother. It made me mad.

I know you're supposed to love your parents, and I do love mine, but sometimes it's just too much. Sometimes my mother is a flake. A genuine, honest-to-goodness, weirdo flake.

Dad's different. He's always had a normal life. He's steady. He's usual. He has a normal job. You knew what he was going to do, at least, until he met Brenda.

Speaking of Brenda, she and Dad drove up just then. As he got out of the car, I saw that Dad was wearing a Banana Republic jacket.

"New duds, hey, Dad?" I asked, as he opened the car door for Brenda.

"Doesn't he look fabulous?" Brenda was saying. "We had the most fun. We spent the whole afternoon at Stilerson's and we got your dad the best clothes." She winked at me. "They were having a sale." She pointed to the pile of boxes in the back of the car. "Wasn't it absolutely the most fun you've ever had in your whole life?" she asked Dad.

"It was fun," he answered.

"But wasn't it absolutely the most fun, I mean, the *most* fun you've ever had?"

"It was fun, Brenda. I had a good time." I think he sighed.

"We got these gorgeous mauve trousers and a chambray shirt and a — "

"Sounds like you bought out the store," Mom said. I was glad she stopped Brenda. I didn't want to hear the list of the fabulous purchases, either. Up till now, Dad usually wore chino slacks and oxford shirts. When he got wild, he'd put on suspenders and a plaid tie.

"Clothes should be *fun*," Brenda was saying to Mom. "Oh, and Julia, Barker's having their early bird sale tomorrow morning. Seven A.M. All belts half price!"

Mom didn't look all that thrilled. "Well, I'm kind of busy getting things packed and all."

"Well, I know, but I thought you'd like to know. You always look so nice, and — "

Dad interrupted her. "Julia," he said. "We've stopped over to get some boxes. Now that the place is sold, I'd better start getting my junk out of the attic."

"But that's going to crowd you," Mom said. "Your apartment's too small."

"You've been to Nat's apartment?" Brenda asked. She drew in her breath, and then she looked embarrassed that she had done it. She pursed her lips.

"Yes, I've been to his apartment lots of times," Mom answered. I really thought I heard a what's-it-to-you tone in her voice.

There was a silence.

"Well, I mean, that's nice," Brenda said. "I knew that you were friendly, but I guess I didn't know that you — " She looked up, as if to make a decision, and then she finished her sentence. "I didn't know that you were *that* friendly."

"I don't see anything wrong with that." This

time, Mom's what's-it-to-you tone was definitely there.

"Well, there's nothing wrong with it, but I — I just didn't know it." Brenda seemed confused. She looked at Dad, but he turned away and started walking toward the house.

Brenda gave him a hurt look. She didn't say anything, but she started making a hole in our lawn with her foot.

"C'mon, Charlie," Dad yelled over his shoulder. "Come help me get some boxes."

Mom called out after him, "But there's no rush, no rush, Nat. I don't want you to feel pressured."

"No, that's okay, I want to make the move as easy for you as possible."

Such consideration, I thought. It made me want to throw up.

Brenda had stopped digging a hole with her shoe and was now actually filling it in and patting down the grass over it. I almost felt sorry for her. She sure looked unhappy.

I went and helped Dad. We were only able to get about four boxes in the trunk and two in the backseat because of all his new clothes.

When we went into the kitchen to get a drink, Mom and Brenda were sitting at the kitchen table having tea.

Mom had brought out the lemon meringue pie she'd made on Monday, and she'd used her favorite china plates. They were sitting there discussing how to teach people with reading problems.

I didn't get it. Twenty minutes ago, Mom was so mad at Brenda, her eyes were turning deep blue. Now, she was serving her a great pie on her special dishes. And they say that kids are confusing!

ELEVEN

The school lunch was responsible for what happened on Friday. When I tried to cut my meatball with a fork, and the meatball oozed, and when I looked at it closer and saw flecks of yellow and green and orange, I decided to skip lunch. I have this weird obsession that I like food to be the color it's supposed to be.

So after school I headed over to Fay's, without Mark this time because he was home sick with a cold. The place was empty when I got there. As I sat down and started looking at the menu, I felt somebody coming over to me, but it was such a hard decision whether to get the burger special or the burger with large fries that I didn't look up. I just said, "I guess I'll have the burger special."

When I didn't hear Fay say her usual, "Certainly, young man," I looked up. I looked straight into the face of David Ransome.

"Fay's out in back for a few minutes," he said. "I can get you a Coke, but you'll have to wait for the burger."

I stared at him. He looked normal. His face wasn't flushed and his teeth weren't bared, and he didn't look as though he was going to smash in my face.

"I don't get it," I told him.

"Whaddaya mean?" he asked.

"I picked a fight with you. I got you in trouble. I got you suspended for a week, and you're not mad at me."

"You were having a bad day."

"Yeah, but — "

"I've been suspended before, it's nothing new." He went to get me my Coke. He filled the glass right to the top. "And — and you did something nobody else has ever done."

I panicked. I thought, What did I do? Oh, no. He's not beating me up because that's too easy. He's going to kill me slowly.

David interrupted my pleasant line of thought. "You apologized."

"I w-what?"

"You apologized. Nobody's ever apologized to me before."

"You kidding?"

"No, they think 'cause I'm dumb they don't have to."

"You're not dumb." He wasn't. Any kid who could have that many people afraid of him without really doing anything was not dumb.

"Tell that to the teachers."

"Well, maybe they're wrong." I took a fast sip of my Coke and spilled some on the counter. I grabbed a napkin to wipe it up.

"They're having me tested next week to find out how dumb I really am," he was saying.

"They can't do that."

"They can. They are. My father says I have to do it. Some shrink's gonna come and test me."

We were quiet. It seemed so unfair.

I didn't know what to say. Just then, Fay came back and she started making my burger. Fay's a big woman. She's tall and heavy, and she has long brown hair tied in a ponytail. She always wears a scarf tied around her forehead. She was humming, like she always does when she's cooking.

David started leaving to go in back, but I asked him if he wanted to have a Coke with me.

"No," he said, "I gotta get to work. I kind of help Fay out."

"Oh, go on," Fay called from the grill. "Get yourself a Coke, David, and sit down with your friend. You need a rest; you've been working too hard."

"You sure?"

"Yes, I'm sure."

David got a Coke and we sat together while I

had my burger. "Tell Charlie about your electronics room," she called.

"Your what?" I asked.

"It's not a room, really," he said. "It's just part of our basement."

"Whaddaya do down there?"

"I got some radio parts and some other stuff, electronic trains. I like to fix 'em. I'm fooling around with soldering some circuit boards now."

"How'd you learn how to do it?"

"Taught myself. My father showed me how to fix a toaster once, and that got me interested."

"I've never done anything like that before."

"If you come over some time, I'll show you."

"Yeah?"

"Yeah." He turned all red then and got up to go. I finished my burger and left, and walked home real slow. I took the long route by Oakland Avenue, looking at all the little houses, each with its own patch of neat lawn, with its own set of matching shrubs in the front.

Then I walked through Franklin Park. I wanted to have it all figured out by the time I got home.

It didn't make any sense. Here was a kid who had one of the biggest thug reputations at school, but he turned out to be grateful for an apology. And to make it more confusing, he was supposed to be dumb, but he played around with electrical circuits for a hobby. Weird.

Even though I walked through Franklin Park twice and then went down Grand and then up Prescott, I still was confused by the time I walked in my door. Then, just by habit, I dialed the phone. Lena answered on the second ring.

I was thinking so hard about David that I forgot about the mall. "You'll never guess what happened."

"What?"

I told her. I told her everything. She couldn't believe it. "Maybe he's one of those geniuses who'll invent great things," she said.

"He invited me over his house."

"You gonna go?"

"I might."

All of a sudden, we got quiet. I remembered that things weren't the same between Lena and me. She must have remembered, just at that moment, too.

"Um, I had a nice time last week," she said.

"You did?"

"Yeah."

"Me, too."

"You know, Central's a big school, Charlie. We probably won't even see each other."

"Yeah."

"Well, we could, like, go to the mall again sometime, maybe."

"Yeah, maybe. I'd like that."

"You would?"

"Yeah."

"Me, too."

I was really glad she said it. She really said, "Me, too." That meant she wanted to see me again.

TWELVE

We're selling our house to the Kazins, the couple with the obnoxious brats, on Wednesday morning, December the ninth, and we're buying our new house right afterward at the same bank. But Mom insisted that she couldn't be ready to move until that Saturday, the twelfth. The Kazins said they couldn't move in until Saturday anyway, so it was arranged that we'd sell them the house officially on Wednesday and then pay them some money so that we could stay for three extra days.

I should have seen it then. Mom wasn't all that busy. We could have moved on Wednesday. But at that point, I wasn't complaining. I liked anything that kept me at Jefferson a few days longer.

I finally got to see our new house when we went over with Adelaide. It was all right. I mean, it was a house. Mom kept raving about the lovely maple in the backyard, and how she'd be able to put up bird feeders. Adelaide kept raving about the beautiful woodwork.

My room was on the second floor. It had two big windows and there was a built-in bookshelf on one wall, but the closet was tiny. There was a Shaker pegboard on another wall for extra clothes. My room was all right. It was a regular room.

After our visit, Mom kept talking about "moving," but she kept buying things for the house, I mean our old house. Like she bought a new Tiffany lamp to hang over our dining room table.

"Hey, Mom," I said. "That's a great lamp. It must of cost a pile."

"I got a good deal on it."

"But will it go in our new place?"

"Oh, no. It's a perfect match here."

"But, Mom, we're moving in a week and a half."

"The move will be fine, don't worry about it, sweetie."

"Mom — "

"You're so much like your father, you're such a worrywart," said she, tousling my hair. I hate it when she does that.

Dad was starting to be over more again. Brenda was taking a course on computers, and she also was working two nights a week. Still, now it felt strange for Dad to be over so much.

It was obvious that he was getting worried about the move. "Julia, do you want me to start picking up boxes for you down at Thompson's?"

"Oh, no, dear, it's much too early to think about that."

The next night it was, "When do you want me to get you some boxes?"

"I hate having them clutter up the house."

The night after that, he just showed up with a pile. Mom took them down into the cellar. Then he did the logical thing. He started bugging *me* about packing *my* room.

"Charlie, you really should get rid of some of this junk."

"What do you mean, junk, Dad?"

"I mean like this Lego set I bought you when you were seven."

"I'm not throwing that away, it could be an antique."

"Don't be ridiculous."

"Remember how Grandma threw away your baseball cards, thinking they were garbage?"

"This is different."

"How? You never know what will become collectible."

"Lego sets? You've got to be kidding."

"Well, it's my room, and I get to decide what to throw away, okay, so don't — "

"Watch your tone, young man."

Why didn't he watch his own tone? Why didn't he stay out of my room?

Mark was over a lot those last few days before we sold the house. While we were packing up a few of my things, we found the old report on Brazil we'd teamed up on in fourth grade. It was in the bottom of my closet.

"This is awful," he said.

"How could we have been so proud of it?"

"Beats me."

"We were awful young."

"And we got a B+ on it."

"Amazing."

"Here, give it to me, I'll toss it."

I gave it to him, and he put it in the trash. We both started at it, sitting in there, and then we both laughed. I took it out of the trash and stuck it in the packing box, next to my stamp collection.

"For old times' sake," I told him.

He nodded.

I didn't get to talk to Lena too much those last few days. With all the confusion, I hardly ever got to use the phone. But I did see David. It was nice to stop over at Fay's after school before going home.

He told me about being tested.

"So what's it like?" I asked him.

"It's not too bad. It's not as bad as I thought it was going to be."

"What are they doing to you?"

"I just gotta take all these weird different tests."

"What's it for?"

"She says to find out my learning style."

"What's that?"

"Who knows, but she says I'm not dumb."

"I could of told you that."

"Yeah, but I wouldn't have believed you, either."

I put my fingers in my Coke and sprayed him good. He grabbed the ketchup and squirted some at me, getting a pile in my Coke. I got him with the mustard. I'd gotten two packages of sugar in his glass and he was on the third in mine before Fay started giving us the "Let's behave, boys. This is a business establishment" looks.

I tried my Coke. Ketchup and sugar hadn't made it too bad. We'd probably invented a great new recipe.

THIRTEEN

Adelaide came over to help on Wednesday after all the legal business was done at the bank. It was official. The Kazins now owned our house, and we owned the house on Elm. The closings had gone off without a hitch. My last hopes had been dashed. I met Adelaide at the door.

"Where is she?" she asked.

I didn't want to tell her, but I had to. "She's painting the bathroom."

"She's what?"

"She's painting the bathroom."

"Why?"

"Ask her, not me."

I heard them from the living room, where I was starting to pack our stereo.

"Julia, why are you painting the bathroom?"

"I've never liked this yellow."

"Julia, you have a whole house to pack, a very

76

full, very large, very stuffed-to-the-gills house to pack."

"Yes, dear, I know."

"Then why are you painting the bathroom?"

"I can't have the Kazins moving in here with this horrible yellow."

"You don't even like the Kazins."

"I never said that."

"Julia, you're a sensible woman. You can paint the bathroom in your new house. Remember, the house you're moving into on Saturday?"

"Oh, yes, of course. Oh, Charlie! Charlie!" she yelled.

I couldn't imagine what she wanted. I was hoping she wanted me to help her get rid of the painting stuff, but no such luck. "Charlie, will you get me the new roller that's on the kitchen table?"

"Mom, you can't paint the bathroom, we've got to move."

"The yellow is — "

"I know. I heard you tell Adelaide. This is so stupid. Even Adelaide knows you're not telling the truth. You just don't want to move."

"That's not true, Charlie!"

"Mom, I'm sick of being the mature one around here. I don't want to move, either. I've never wanted to move, but I know we have to."

"As soon as I finish this, I'll start packing."

"You'll start another *project*."

"That's not fair. I know the house is sold. I know

the Kazins are moving in on Saturday."

"Mom, I'm not saying you're crazy."

"You're saying that we have to be out of here on Saturday."

"At noon."

"High noon," she agreed.

I wished her saying that made me feel better, but it didn't. I had this sick feeling that nothing we were saying was making any difference. Mom just had this odd look on her face. When Mom got that look on her face, I knew there was no hope of reasoning with her.

Adelaide was still trying. She was saying, "Why can't you just finish the wall you're doing and stop there?"

"But it's half done. I might as well finish the whole thing."

Adelaide and I looked at each other. She knew Mom pretty well, too. "All right, but then no more new projects, right?"

"Yes, dear, of course. I wouldn't think of it."

Adelaide and I conferred in the living room. "She's obviously having a problem with this move," she said.

"That may be the understatement of the century."

"Well, look, we're capable people. We can pack this house in three days."

"Two," I said.

"Two?"

"Wednesday's almost gone. Besides, I'm supposed to go to school, remember?"

"What difference does it make? You're going to a new school, they'll never know the difference."

"I want to go to school this week."

"What is this, a personality transformation?" She knew me pretty well, too.

"It's my last two days at Jefferson. Look, I'm the one who's supposed to be having a crisis here, not my mother. My mother's not the one who has to change schools. My mother's not the one who's going to have to be a new kid all over again."

"I'm sorry, Charlie, you're right. But look, we've got tonight, and your father will be over around five. C'mon, let's stop talking and get to it. I'll go start on the studio, and you keep doing what you were doing before."

"Packing the stereo."

"Fine," said Adelaide.

I did go and pack the stereo. I stuffed Styrofoam around the speakers, and when the pieces didn't quite fit, I jammed them down into the box. It felt good to scrunch something, to scrunch something really hard.

Dad arrived about five-fifteen. He came right over after work with a pile of boxes. Mom was still in the bathroom, painting like mad. He took one look at her and came out to talk to me.

"We have to have a plan," he said.

"What do you mean, 'we'? I don't want to move, remember?"

"Charles, your mother is in a state."

"So, I'm in a state, too, Dad."

"But your mother is in a bigger one."

I knew it was true. I couldn't deny it. I felt really mad, but I knew I had no choice. My mother was in a bad way, and I was probably going to have to cooperate. I didn't say anything. What could I say? I just went back to my packing and tried to ignore my mother, who, by then, was taking all the chairs out of the kitchen so she could wash and wax the kitchen floor.

My father wasn't even trying to reason with her. I just saw him and Adelaide talking in the garage. I knew they were planning strategies.

FOURTEEN

Things. I used to collect things, too. Everybody does around here.

I'm going to break my own personal rule of writing, the one about never writing descriptions. Be honest, when you're reading along, and you come to a long description, don't you say to yourself, "Yuck!"?

Sometimes, I make myself start reading the description, but I usually wind up skipping the whole thing. They take so long.

Probably when people didn't have televisions and stereos, it was different. Probably then, they sat down on a Friday night and said, "Yippee, let's read this long description, and let's savor every word. We have until the candle goes out to finish this chapter." It made sense then. Not now.

But I have to describe our house so you'll know what we were up against. Our house is big, and my mother is not exactly against material possessions. In fact, my mother is a Collector. Not a collector of bottles or seashells or antique furniture. My mother is a collector of everything!

I'll start with our living room. It's a big room with high ceilings and exposed beams. It's too bad that some of the beams have spaces above them, because Mom has things even up there: old bottles, ceramic figures of little girls and boys, vases of dried flowers. Mom even has old pottery jugs up there, the kind that people oooooh and aaaaah about — the ones that antique dealers claim are worth a lot of money, but nobody ever buys. My mother does, and she hauls them up to the beams in our living room.

We haven't even talked about the walls yet. When I was in third grade, I made the big mistake of doing some stupid little paintings of my dog Sammy (who died soon after) and some flowers in the backyard (they died, too). I did a picture of Superman, who was then my superhero. My mother framed all the pictures and put them on our living room wall.

Well, I begged Mom to take the pictures down, because Sammy was hit by a car, and I blamed Superman. I was convinced that he was supposed to have saved my dog.

I would have torn down the pictures, especially the one of the big fake in the cape costume, but they were too high for me. One day, Mom caught me just as I was trying to smash it with a rock.

Then we had a "talk," and she finally got the idea that I really hated Superman and that I didn't like seeing my dead dog staring at me from the living room wall, either. So she took those pictures down and I figured that I was finally free of them.

But then a year ago, she casually asked if I still blamed Superman for Sammy's death. When I told her that of course I didn't, that I blamed the jerk in the car that hit him, the pictures showed up on the walls again. Mom said that they were wonderful "primitives" and that they showed "real creative interest." Big deal.

Most parents take pictures their kids draw and put them up for a while, stick them up on the refrigerator or on the bathroom wall for a few days. Then, the first chance they get, when the kid's not looking, they chuck the pictures in the trash, which is where they belong.

Sometimes my mother is a real flake. She's saved everything I've ever made.

I wandered around the house Thursday morning, looking at all the stuff that Dad and Adelaide were going to have to pack. Then I went to school.

By then, news had gotten out that I was going to move, and a few kids came over to say goodbye. Even old Mr. Vincini stopped me in the halls and wished me good luck.

Mr. Aberdinian, *the* Mr. Aberdinian, the one that I thought hated me, said it was too bad I had to go.

"Stop by and see us sometime," he said.

"Sure." I didn't tell him that I might not ever be gone.

Thursday took forever. I got home that afternoon to find Adelaide and Mom in a fight. I heard their voices as soon as I started coming up our walk.

"What are you doing?" Mom was screaming. By then, I was close enough to see Adelaide stuffing a box of old *National Geographic*s in the trash.

"Oh, do you need them?"

"Need them, of course I need them! They're a very important part of my filing system."

"What filing system?"

"I have all the articles listed alphabetically."

"You don't."

"I do."

"Why?"

"I may need the information some day."

"This is the most ridiculous — "

"I hope they're not damaged. Here, get me the Scotch tape. This one's cover has been ripped. You must have ripped it when you — "

"It was ripped when I took it out of the box."

"They were all perfect."

"It was ripped. Ripped. RIPPED!" Adelaide was screaming. Then suddenly she got quiet, very quiet. And then she started grabbing all the magazines out of Mom's hands and ripping their covers and their pages.

Mom got calm. "Adelaide, look at me. Adelaide,

please calm down. I want you to be reasonable."

"Be reasonable? You haven't been reasonable in days, in weeks!" Adelaide was still shouting and ripping.

"You're having a fit. Take a deep breath."

"A deep breath? I need more than a deep breath." She was still ripping.

"Calm down, Adelaide!" Mom was starting to yell.

"No!"

"Stop ripping my magazines!"

"No! I *love* ripping your magazines."

"Give them to me!"

"NO!"

"Give them to me!"

I thought they were going to have a fight. I thought I was going to have a break up a genuine fistfight between my mother and her best friend.

I tried to figure out which one I'd hold down. But that wouldn't work because I could tell from the looks on their faces that if I held one of them back, the other one would let her have it.

So I got in between them. It shocked them, and they stopped yelling and stood there, staring at each other.

Then Adelaide mumbled something and went into the kitchen. She was crying.

"Hey, so don't feel so bad," I told her later. "Everybody loses it once in a while."

"I just don't know what to *do* with her. She's

not letting me pack. She emptied all the boxes of kitchen stuff I packed this morning before I knew what she was doing.''

''Why?''

''She said she had to make supper.''

''She's gone totally wacko.''

''I'm afraid to leave her alone. Whatever I do, she undoes.'' She was quiet for a minute. ''Hey, Charlie.''

''I won't do it.''

''C'mon, Charlie. Just for tonight.''

I knew what she wanted. She wanted me to keep my mother busy so that she and Dad could pack. I figured that wasn't one of the duties I signed up for when I became a son.

I know I have to make a big deal out of Mother's Day, and I know the deal about love and respect and all that. But nowhere does it say that I have to baby-sit my mother who's gone nuts because she's having to move when she doesn't want to, and she doesn't want to admit it.

Besides, I don't want to move, either. Everybody, everybody in this whole house, is forgetting about that!

FIFTEEN

I didn't go to school on Friday. Thursday night was too hard. I kept reminding myself that it wasn't fair, that I was the one who was getting ignored.

What difference did it make to my mother if she moved across town? Her job was the same. Her friends were the same. She just looked at a different set of trees when she was having coffee in the morning.

I was going to have to switch schools, just when I was finally getting to know the ropes. And with David and me being friends, nobody ever bothered me anymore.

But my mother was in sad shape. Even my father had this serious look on his face that I'd only seen once before, when I'd had appendicitis and they were rushing me to the hospital.

Dad took the day off to help us pack, and I stayed home, in spite of myself.

We had boxes in the living room and boxes in the halls, and Mom wouldn't touch them. And she wouldn't let us touch them, or so she thought. We outsmarted her, her old friend Adelaide and her old ex-husband and her supposedly too-young-to-know-how-to-do-it son. As desperate as she was, we were even more desperate.

We had a special trick. Adelaide would hold up one of Mom's favorite possessions. By eleven o'clock Friday morning, Mom defined all of her possessions as favorites, so Adelaide had lots of ammunition. Anyway, Adelaide would hold up a precious piece and say to Mom, "This can just go in with that box of garden tools, don't you think, Julia?"

Mom would immediately become hysterical. "Don't you dare. That's my favorite tulip vase. Give it to me. Give it to me, now."

After they had tugged and pulled at it for a while, Adelaide would suddenly look up and say, "Of course, dear, pack it where you like. It's such a gorgeous vase for tulips."

In those few minutes, I was able to grab the Satsumi lamp from off the marble top, pack four china cups with saucers, and start a new box full of teapots. Mom had lots of teapots. I was getting very fast at packing.

"What are you doing, Charlie?" asked Mom.

Adelaide saw a problem, so she acted. "Oh, Julia,

don't you think we could just throw this out?"

"Throw it out, are you crazy? That's my *best* gravy bowl."

I found the boxes of rocks at 4:47. I was standing in Mom's studio, looking at her storage unit, which was attached to the wall. It was taller than me and at least fourteen feet long, and it was loaded with neatly labeled boxes. I read, EXTRA SOLDER, PIGEON FEATHERS, STERLING SILVER EARWIRES, CHICKEN BONES. Chicken bones? Sure enough, it was a box full of clean chicken bones. How can you use chicken bones in making silver jewelry?

Since the boxes were all packed, I thought Dad and I could just load them in the truck. Adelaide was harrassing Mom upstairs, so I figured we had a good fifteen minutes of freedom.

Dad and I started carrying out the boxes, and I just grabbed one on the bottom without thinking. I almost broke my back. Then I looked at the label, which said ROCKS.

"Look at this, Dad. She's saved rocks."

"I'd believe anything at this point."

Sure enough, we opened the box, and there was a pile of rocks. They were pretty, all different kinds, but they were rocks. Not pebbles, rocks. Dad and I looked at each other, and I could tell by the smile that came into his eyes that we were thinking the same thought.

"Hey, Dad."

"We shouldn't."

"Why not?"

"She'll know. I don't know how, but she'll know."

We sat on the floor, not looking at each other. Then he said, "I don't care."

"You don't?"

"No, not a whit."

"Me, neither."

It was great. We'd thrown out at least fifteen boxes in the woods behind our house before Mom escaped from Adelaide to find out what we were doing. I'd even gotten rid of the chicken bones and four boxes of pinecones.

Dad was heading to the backyard with another big load of rocks when Mom came running out of the house. We would have been caught for sure, but just then Brenda drove up.

She got out of the car and walked over to us. "Hi, Julia," she said, "Hi, Charlie." Then she turned to Dad. "When will you be finished up here, Nat?"

"I'm not sure, it's — "

"Well, will you be done by six? You know, Hal and Jennifer expect us at seven."

"Brenda, I probably won't. Julia really needs my help."

"Why? I don't understand."

"You just go on ahead. Tell Hal and Jennifer I'm sorry, that something came up."

"But, Nat, we had a date. We're supposed to go over there together. This isn't like you at all."

"I know, Brenda, I'm sorry, but Julia really needs my help."

"But what about me? What about Hal and Jennifer? We told them we'd be there."

"She needs my help."

Brenda stood there, looking at him. She started digging a hole in our lawn with her foot, like she'd done the last time she'd been over, but then she stopped herself. She looked long and hard at Dad, and then she turned away.

"Brenda, I'm sorry," Dad said. He sounded really sorry.

"I think I'm starting to understand," she answered.

I was glad that *she* did. *I* didn't understand at all.

"Brenda?" Dad asked.

"Yeah?"

"C'mon, let's go for a ride around the block."

"Are you sure you want to?"

"I am."

They both got in the car and drove away, leaving me and Mom standing there. I suddenly realized that Mom hadn't said a word throughout the whole thing. She suddenly turned away and went back in the house. She didn't even look in the boxes that Dad had left on the lawn.

I picked up the boxes and brought them in the

back and threw the rocks out in the woods like we'd done with the others. Somehow, though, it wasn't as much fun as before.

I went back into the house and tried to call Lena, but the line was busy. I tried for the next half hour, with no luck. Things were terrific all around.

Sixteen

By six o'clock, the U-Haul was still sitting in the driveway, mostly empty except for a wall of boxes and a couple of end tables. It had been quiet after Brenda's visit.

Mark stopped over, and he couldn't believe how little we'd gotten packed. It really was pretty hard to believe.

"You know, maybe you won't have to move, after all," he said.

Just then the phone rang. It was Lena. I told her what was happening.

"Wow," she said. "Maybe you won't have to move."

"Yeah, but the house is sold," I told her.

"Yeah, but your mother won't move," she told me.

"Yeah, but the cops will probably come and drag us out," I answered.

"Well, then you can go and live with Mark," she said.

I turned to Mark, who was standing right next to me. "Lena says I should come and live with you."

"Wow. That's *great*. How come we didn't think of that before?"

"I don't know. But could I?"

"Could you what?"

"Live with you if I have to."

"Sure."

"You mean it?"

"Yeah, it'd be *great*."

"But what about your parents?"

"They won't mind," Mark assured me. "They like you."

"Wow."

Mark and I stood there looking at each other, until I finally remembered that Lena was still on the phone.

"Lena," I said, "you're brilliant."

"Actually, I prefer to think of myself as a creative genius," she said, and we both laughed.

Mom and Adelaide came in just then, so I got off the phone. I didn't want to talk about our backup plan in front of them.

Mom had been taking a little nap. When she'd woken up, she suddenly decided that she wanted to write to her friend Martha, who'd moved to California.

"Tell her hi for me," Adelaide said. She winked at me.

I knew what she was thinking. She was figuring that at least Mom would be out of our hair.

"What have you done with Martha's address?" Mom yelled to me.

"Nothing, Mom. I haven't touched it." For once, I was telling the truth.

"I *know* it's here somewhere."

"I haven't *touched* it."

"I know you're throwing out my things," she said.

"I'm *not!*" I lied. I figured it was only a little lie, because I'd only been throwing out her junk things. Besides, why was I getting blamed when Dad and Adelaide had probably thrown out more of her stuff than I had? Kids get blamed for everything!

Mom ran off to search for the address, and Adelaide asked Mark and me to help her carry a table from the cellar. We helped her. It was a habit by then. Most of me didn't believe we'd move, but Adelaide looked so tired, I just found myself helping her.

We were lifting the table into the truck when we found Mom. She was sitting inside the moving truck, unpacking boxes. She was unpacking the few measly boxes that we'd managed to get into the truck. There was newspaper and junk spread all around.

Poor Adelaide. "Julia, what are you doing?"

"I have to find Martha's address. I have something very important to tell her. Now, where is — "

"Julia — "

"Adelaide — "

"What, Charlie," she asked.

"It's no use."

She knew I was right. Then I got a good idea. "Hey, Mom, wouldn't it be better to just call her?"

"But her number — "

"You can get it from Information. C'mon, I'll help."

She went with me. We got Martha's number, and we got Martha on the phone. They talked for half an hour. Mom didn't say anything about moving.

The only thing that I was mad about was that I hadn't thought of the telephoning idea earlier. We could have kept her on the phone with all her friends from around the country. It would have been expensive, but it would have been worth it.

By Friday night, it was too late. We just couldn't fight her anymore. She'd won.

I don't know why Adelaide stayed. I mean, I know about her and Mom being best friends, but I'm not sure I would have done this even for Mark.

For that matter, I don't know why Dad stayed. He'd been gone with Brenda for about an hour, and when he got back, he'd been quiet. He'd been more than quiet. He didn't even hear me a couple of times when I talked to him. That wasn't like him at all.

Then Brenda showed up again around seven-thirty and they went off together. She didn't even get out of the car the last time. She didn't even drive in the driveway. She just parked out in front and blew the horn until Dad came out.

By then Adelaide and I knew that Mom wasn't going to make it. The Kazins were coming tomorrow at noon, with two kids, and from the looks of them, probably a ton of furniture, and Mom was going to be in their house. Worse than that, Mom's furniture was going to be in their house.

I considered going over to Mark's that night and staying there, but I just couldn't do it. Mark understood. Mark was terrific. He just stayed with me and didn't talk too much. He called his mom and she said that he could stay over.

So we just stopped and had supper. Mom made spaghetti and a big salad, and we had apple pie for dessert. We were quiet, very quiet.

The funny thing is, Mom actually packed a couple of boxes after supper. There we were, all sitting around the kitchen table, not saying much, and she just got up and packed a box of her dishes. I'll admit, they were the ones that Grandma gave her two Christmases ago, which she hates, but she actually packed them. Mark and Adelaide and I just sat there and watched her. We didn't say anything.

Then she started packing the aluminum pots that she never uses.

"Maybe if we'd just left you alone, you would have packed more than all of us together," Adelaide said.

"What do you mean? You got a lot done."

"But don't you realize how much is left?"

"We have tomorrow morning."

"We've only packed half the study and Charlie's room and part of your workshop."

"There're lots of things gone from the living room," said Mom, "like the Satsumi lamp and Charlie's paintings."

"Pictures, Mom, pictures. They aren't good enough to be called paintings."

"You've never had enough confidence in yourself. By the way, where did you pack them?"

"Carefully, Mom, very carefully." I wasn't going to tell her that I threw them in the garbage yesterday afternoon.

"But, Julia," Adelaide said, "don't you realize that we haven't even touched the kitchen?"

"Now, that's not right. I've just packed Grandma's dishes and those horrible aluminum pots."

"But look at all the other stuff in here."

It wasn't that we hadn't had this conversation before. We'd had this conversation at least eighty-five times in the past three days. But this time, *we* had changed. We weren't trying to get her to do anything anymore. We knew she wouldn't.

"Let's play Boggle," she said.

"I hate Boggle, let's play Monopoly," said Adelaide.

"It's got to be a gin rummy night," I said.

And that it was. We played gin rummy, and then we played poker. We even played old maid with a deck we found in Mom's desk. We had a good time. This is a bizarre thing to say, but we actually had a good time.

It got to be about eleven-thirty and Adelaide went home. Mark slept on the couch in the living room. I was really glad that he stayed.

SEVENTEEN

I woke up late the next morning. Mark was already up, having leftover apple pie in the kitchen.

"What can they do to us?" I asked him.

"Maybe arrest you for trespassing?" he answered.

"But we're not really *trespassing*."

"But you're where you're not supposed to be."

"Yeah, in our own home." We laughed. It was *slightly* funny. "Maybe they can arrest us for disorderly conduct," I went on.

"Maybe they have a special crime called 'Failure to Move Out of a House You've Sold.' "

"You think so?"

"They might."

"But they can't send me to jail. I'm a minor. They can only send my mom." Somehow that wasn't a very comforting thought.

Mark made me feel even worse. "But they can send you to reform school."

I groaned. We both groaned.

"I'd hide you in my basement first," he said.

I felt a little better when he said that.

Dad showed up around ten-thirty, and when Mom got up, we all sat around the kitchen table, having coffee. I even had half a cup and Mom didn't say anything. I figured it was a special occasion. It was my last day of freedom. I'd probably be on bread and water at reform school, or eating whatever crumbs Mark could sneak down to me in his basement.

Dad was different. He was still quiet, but he seemed calmer than he'd been for days, weeks. I couldn't remember the last time I'd seen him look so settled, determined. I couldn't figure out how he looked, but it was different.

When Mr. Kazin drove in with his U-Haul, we were still sitting in the kitchen.

"Stay here," Dad said to us, and we obeyed. He had that tone. He went out to the yard to talk to Mr. Kazin.

Mr. Kazin was mad. He got out of the truck, and from the window we could see him waving his arms, and it seemed like he was yelling. Dad just kept standing there, talking to him.

Mrs. Kazin got out of the truck and then she started waving her arms, but Dad just kept standing there, talking to them.

After a while, the Kazins' arms got less active, and then they both stood there talking to Dad. Then the weirdest thing happened: Mrs. Kazin went over to Mr. Kazin and gave him a big hug, and then he gave her a big kiss, and then they both shook hands with Dad, and Mrs. Kazin actually kissed him on the cheek, and they got back into the U-Haul and drove off. I can't be sure, but I think I heard Mr. Kazin yell "Good luck" to Dad as they drove off. It was bizarre.

I'd expected more to happen. I thought there was going to be a big fight with the Kazins. I'd also expected cops and attendants carrying straitjackets and sirens blaring and lights flashing, just like on television. What really happened was that we were left with silence. We all just sat there, watching the Kazins pull out of our driveway.

Dad came back into the kitchen. "C'mon, Julia," he said. "We're leaving."

"What?"

"We're leaving. Remember when we went to Riverside that day?"

"But we were kids. That was before we were married."

"Well, we're going there again."

"What for?"

"To have some fun. I'm taking you to Riverside this afternoon and we're going to ride the roller coaster, and then I'm taking you out to supper to that new Mexican restaurant in Hadley."

"But —"

"No buts, get your stuff and let's go."

"Dad?"

"What, Charlie?"

"What are you doing?"

"I'm taking your mother out."

"Why?"

"She needs to get out of here for a while. I should have done it days ago."

"But what about the Kazins?"

"They've given us a week's extension."

"They have?"

"Yes."

"Why?"

"I asked them to."

"They said yes, just like that?"

"When I explained things."

"Does that mean we still have to move?"

"Yes, Charlie, by next Saturday."

"Oh."

"Charlie," Dad said, "I know it's confusing, but don't worry about it, I know what I'm doing. I finally know what I'm doing."

"Well, do you want us to pack up the place while you're gone, or what?"

"No, Charlie, don't pack. Your mother and I have a lot of talking to do."

Great. Here my mother had successfully not moved on moving day, and now my father was taking her out on a date. I wonder what it would be like to have normal parents.

And what was happening about Brenda? From

the little I'd seen of her yesterday, she hadn't looked too happy. I know I'm not supposed to feel sorry for my father's fiancée, but ever since I'd put that ant in her Coke — years ago, it seemed — I had sort of liked her more. It looked like Brenda was getting a raw deal.

Did Dad taking Mom out on a date mean that he'd broken up with Brenda? What was going on, anyway?

Mark and I hung around and watched TV. Then we finished the leftover spaghetti from last night, and then we had a water fight with the dish sprayer in the kitchen. Our hearts weren't in it. It wasn't that much fun.

Then we took the bus to the mall. We went right to the game room and played video games for three hours straight. I blew all my money. Then we walked around the mall a few hundred times, and then Mark treated me to a burger and fries at Friendly's. It helped.

EIGHTEEN

I went to school on Monday. Mrs. Martinelli, my homeroom teacher, gave me a hard time about being there.

"Charles, you're not on my rolls."

"Well, I'm here."

"Why are you here?"

"We haven't moved yet."

"When are you going to move?"

"I don't know. Maybe never." There was laughter from the class.

"Is this a joke, Charles?"

"No, really, Mrs. Martinelli. I really don't know."

"Well, I'd better check with the office." Just then the first-period bell rang. "All right, go on to class and I'll check on this later."

Things were normal until third period. The halls had the same old dirty-sneaker smell, and my locker was still stuck, and the paint was still peeling off the walls in the science room. Things were the same at school. Nothing was the same at home.

Things were the same, that is, until third period. Mark and I were walking to History when Harold Thompson stepped out from the wall. He said it quietly. That's what got me off guard.

"Heard your mother's cracking up."

"What?"

"So they going to take her away in a straitjacket or what?"

"Shut your lousy mouth!" I don't know how it happened, but I had him by the throat.

"Hey, Charlie, just ignore him, he's a jerk!" Mark was trying to help, but something about the smug look on Harold's face made me want to pound his nose into mush.

I figured if he knew about my mother, the whole school knew, and they'd been laughing at me all day. Worse than that, they'd been laughing at my mother.

I slugged Harold in the gut, but then I felt these arms holding me from behind. Harold was cowering, doubled over in front of me, and Mark was standing between us, so I didn't know who was holding me.

"Hey, man, cool it. I thought you'd given this up." It was David. He had a firm hold on my arms.

I kept struggling to get at Harold. I felt strong enough to send him to the plastic surgeons. "Let me go, let me at him."

David just held on. Since he still had the body

of a freight train, there was nothing I could do, and Harold took off.

"C'mon, lemme at him."

David just held on, and I started to calm down. I started to remember that, by nature, I wasn't a violent person.

"How'd he know about it?" I asked. "How could he know about it?"

From the way David and Mark looked at each other, I knew. They didn't even have to tell me, but they did.

Mark said, "When you weren't in on Friday, David and I were talking about it in the gym. We didn't think anybody was there, but we walked around the corner, and we saw Harold standing there, smirking."

"I'm sorry, Charlie," David said.

I got mad again. Why did they have to talk about me behind my back? But then I remembered how I'd done something really stupid to David at the beginning of the year, how I'd even gotten him suspended for a week. He'd accepted my apology. And here he was, apologizing to me.

"It's okay, Dave," I said.

"I'm sorry, too, Charlie," Mark said. "We would of never said anything if we knew Harold was there."

"It's okay, let's just forget about it." As soon as I'd said it, I remembered my other awful thought. "Did he tell anybody else about it?"

"He might of, with his big mouth."

"You know, I don't want to hurt your feelings or anything," Mark said, "but most of the kids just don't care if your mom's acting weird."

I know he said it to make me feel better, but it didn't.

"C'mon, let me go, I'll be all right."

"Y'know, I think we should make you promise," Mark said.

"C'mon, I'll be all right."

David finally let me go. I sagged. I felt like *I'd* just been beaten up.

I went through the rest of the day like a robot, not looking right or left. I didn't talk to anybody, and I kept my head down so nobody would talk to me. I didn't want anybody asking me about my mother.

Nobody said anything. People left me alone. On the outside, it seemed like just a normal day.

Mark and I went over to Fay's after school and talked to David for a few minutes. Then we walked around town for a while, not saying much. I knew that he really wanted to go home, but he didn't know what to do about me. I knew that I definitely wasn't going home.

"You know, you don't have to be my body-guard," I told him. "I promise I won't beat on any little kid that passes by."

"What if Harold passes by?"

"He won't. Did you see how scared he was?"

He laughed. "Yeah, that was pretty good. For a former wimp, you're getting quite a reputation."

"Yeah, I could probably win an award for increasing my violence level."

"An 'Excellence in Thug Development' award."

We laughed, but not too hard. Neither one of us liked it. I wasn't proud of myself, slugging Harold. Something about that scared look on his face made me feel sick to my stomach.

"I guess I should of told him to shut up and then I should of walked away," I said. "I'm getting too old to be belting people every time they say something I don't like."

"Probably."

We walked in silence. Then Mark said, "You want to have supper at my house?"

It was a nice offer. Mark was a good friend. But something inside me had changed during our talk, and I knew I had to turn him down. "No thanks. I think I'm going to go home and see what's happening."

"You sure?"

"Yeah."

"If you want to come over later, just come on."

"Yeah. Hey, Mark?"

"What?"

"Thanks."

NINETEEN

The house was empty, completely empty. All our stuff was still there, but Mom and Dad were nowhere to be seen.

I wandered from room to room. Except for the few things Adelaide and Dad and I had been able to pack last week, everything was the same.

The phone rang. It was Mrs. Schneider, and she was speaking in a crisp voice.

"Your mother there?"

"Hello," I said politely.

"Oh, hello, hello. I said, is your mother there?"

"She's not home at the present. May I ask who's calling?" I was really pouring it on.

"You know who this is. I demand to speak to your mother."

"I'm sorry, but she's not home."

She hung up. I was hoping she wouldn't show

110

up in person, because this was one adult whom I didn't want to deal with alone.

I went into the kitchen and ate the rest of the baked chicken and the leftover pizza Mom and Dad had brought back last night. Then I finished off the Oreo cookies and the Doritos. I was starting on the half gallon of butter pecan when Mom and Dad got home. They were laughing and holding hands. As soon as they walked into the kitchen, Mrs. Schneider drove up.

She knocked once and then stormed into the house. "You haven't moved a stick of furniture. I can see that you haven't even moved a *stick* of furniture. It's awful what you're doing to those people."

Mom interrupted her. "Haven't you spoken to the Kazins?"

"No. They left a message on my answering machine that they've given you another week. You're taking complete advantage of them and I will not have it! When I sell a house, I — "

"Did they say *why* they're giving us the extra week?"

"No. I can see why. You haven't moved a *stick of furniture!*"

"Mrs. Schneider, please give us just a moment to explain." Something about the way Mom said it made Mrs. Schneider stop and listen. It made me stop and listen, too.

Mom went on. "Nat and I have been fooling ourselves. We've been fooling ourselves for years. Charlie knew it, Charlie knew it when he was eight years old."

"Mom, what are you talking about?"

"Honey, you told us when you were eight years old that none of your friends' parents who were divorced acted like we did. You said that if Dad was over here all the time, and if we liked each other as much as we obviously did, that we should just get remarried and stop pretending that we were divorced."

"I did? I said that?"

"Yes."

I didn't remember it at all, but I must have been a pretty smart kid. Then it dawned on me what Mom was really saying. "Do you mean, do you mean you and Dad are getting married?"

"Yes, it does, Charlie," Dad answered. "This whole moving thing, this whole move has made me realize, it's made me realize so much." He looked at Mom. "All I can say is, I'm *glad* you can't make a move without me, Julia."

"Go on," Mom answered. "I can make plenty of moves without you. But this time, I'm making the *right* move." I think she giggled.

Mrs. Schneider was still standing there. All the air seemed to have escaped from her body. She looked deflated, but she didn't look angry anymore. In fact, she was starting to look a little pleased. "Well, this certainly is big news," she said. "This is certainly big news. But does that mean — " She stopped, but Mom seemed to know what she was going to ask.

"No, Mrs. Schneider, we sold the house in good faith to the Kazins, and we really will be out by next week. We've hired movers to come in on Wednesday and move us out. We actually should be out of here by Thursday evening."

"Actually, Mrs. Schneider," Dad said, "in a funny way, it's probably better that we're moving to a new place. I think we need a new start."

"Well, this is, this is so, so romantic. This is wonderful." Mrs. Schneider was actually sputtering. "I mean, after all these years, you decided to get married again because of selling the house?"

"That's it. That's what happened."

"Well, I'll have to tell my husband. He always says, he always calls me such a matchmaker, and, and I really feel that I had a part, I had a part in all this. This is just so, so *romantic*."

We all laughed, and even Mrs. Schneider laughed when she realized how much she was oooohing and aaaaahing.

"Well, when are you getting married, and who's making your cake, and . . . I insist that you invite me to your wedding."

"Well, yes, if you want to come," said my mother.

"Oh, that will be so delightful, and I'll wear my

new beige silk, and my husband will just be thrilled when I tell him."

Mrs. Schneider finally left half an hour later, after she and her husband had been promised an invitation. By that time, she'd planned the whole wedding. Bernstein's would cater, and Letterman's would do the flowers, and Mom would buy her dress at Harvenson's. On and on she went. Mrs. Schneider obviously loved weddings.

When she'd finally gone, I asked, "What about Brenda?"

"Brenda knows," Dad said. "We've talked for hours. This whole thing hasn't been fair to her, but it would have been even worse for me to marry her when I realized I was still in love with your mom."

"Why didn't you know that before?"

"I don't know. Stupidity, I guess. But Brenda will be okay, Charlie. She understands, and she'll be okay. She's a fine person. She'll find someone else in time."

"You've caused all this trouble. I mean, we could have just stayed here. Now I'm going to have to change schools, and — " I started going into my you've-caused-me-all-this-trouble-and-you-are-such-stupid-parents routine, but the look on Mom's face stopped me. She looked happy.

"Charlie, you were right all along," Dad said. "We should of gotten remarried years ago."

"But it'll never work. You're so different. You've both said so."

"We're not saying it's going to be a normal life."

Mom grabbed Dad and kissed him. Then she made a grab for me, but I was too fast. She didn't catch me until I slipped on the rug in the living room and almost tripped. That slowed me down.

"Well, I guess we've never had a normal life before, so why start now?" I said.

TWENTY

The movers came right on time. It took them two days to pack and move the stuff, even with Dad and me helping. He'd taken the week off from work. Mom went over to Adelaide's and stayed with her.

The movers plopped everything in the new house, and we started the big job of unpacking. Dad didn't say anything to me about starting school, and I didn't mention the issue. As far as I was concerned, I could miss it until next year.

"Hey, Dad."

"What, Charlie?"

"Are you sorry, I mean, all this trouble? Are you sorry that we just didn't stay in our old house?"

"Well, we both know what a pain it was, but this feels better. This feels like we'll really get a new start."

Dad and I spent a day putting stuff away. Mom

116

decided she could face it on Saturday morning and she showed up with Adelaide around eleven. All she said was, "Oh, dear, I didn't realize we had so much junk."

"We?" I queried.

"Well, you have all that — "

"C'mon, Mom."

"Well, I . . . what's this?" She was opening the box that had the pile of old telephone books.

"Mom, those have old, important telephone numbers in them, remember? You wouldn't let me throw them away."

"Well, but they're not current. I'm sure I don't need them anymore."

I looked over at Dad and Adelaide, and for a moment they looked as mad as I felt. Mom kept opening other boxes and saying things like, "This stuff is just junk, it's just got to go, I can't imagine why you let the movers bring this stuff." She went on and on.

That's when I learned that I still had a sense of humor, because at that very moment, I started to laugh.

"What are you laughing about?"

"It's just so, so, so . . ."

Dad and Adelaide and I rolled on the floor, with Mom looking on as though we were nuts.

"Go to it, Mom," I said. "Throw away as much junk as you want." I grabbed a couple of boxes that I knew had my things, because I didn't trust her, the mood she was in.

She did throw stuff away. She went through box after box for a week. It was amazing. That's when I figured that maybe Dad and she had a shot at making it after all. I mean, who knows about adults? They're stranger than kids.

She did ask about the rocks, though, the ones we'd thrown out in the woods. She wanted to make a rock garden in the backyard.

We pleaded ignorance. We told her the movers must have thrown them out.

Saturday afternoon, I rode my bike over to Mark's and we walked over to Fay's to see David. David told us the most amazing news. The lady who'd tested him had decided that he needed to go to a special program. It was for kids with learning disabilities. It was in Central, my new school.

"You going to do it?" I asked him.

"My father's going to make me."

"Yeah, but that's great! That means we're going to the *same school*."

"Far out!"

A couple of months ago, it would have been my worst nightmare to have David transfer to Central. Now I was glad. Now he was a friend.

Then I noticed that Mark wasn't saying much. I didn't blame him. Now he wasn't even going to have David at Jefferson.

"Well, we'll go to high school together," I told

him. At least both Central and Jefferson feed into Pioneer High.

"That's not for three years," he said.

It did seem forever, but I didn't feel like being sad. "C'mon," I told them. "Let's go to the mall. Does Fay need you to help, Dave?"

"No, it's slow. I'm just hanging around anyway."

Just for old times' sake, we took David into The Limited and saw the Lena girl. Her hair was purple now.

"Nice hair," I told her.

"Thanks. Hey, weren't two of you in here a while ago?"

"Not us," I said. "We live in Texas. We're just visiting for the weekend. You must be thinking of somebody else."

"You look awful familiar," she said.

"Lots of people tell me that," I told her, smiling. "I think I have a common face."

"Hey, I remember, you're the kid that came in here and almost broke the jewelry case."

"No, I live in Texas. You're thinking of somebody else."

"Go on . . ."

"I'm just not the same kid."

"Well, maybe. You need any help?"

"No thanks, we're just looking around for a present for my girlfriend."

"You mean that girl over there?"

"Huh?"

She pointed over to the sweater rack, where a girl was standing and staring at me. I almost gasped. I almost gasped because when I looked up, I was staring straight into the face of Lena, the real Lena.

"Hi," she said.

"Hi," I said. "I'm here with Mark and David. This is Mark and this is Dave."

"Oh," she said.

"Nice to meet you," they said.

The Lena girl yelled over, "Pretty nice girlfriend you've got there!" She winked.

"Let's get out of here," I told everyone, and then I just blurted out, almost by accident, "Hey, Lena, want to go get a Coke?"

She looked embarrassed, but then she looked me straight in the eye and said, "Yes. I don't have to meet my mom for another hour."

We all went to Friendly's. It was kind of weird at first, but pretty soon we were all laughing and joking. It felt like I'd known Lena for years, in person, I mean.

Lena and I decided that we'd act normal at school. If we saw each other, we'd talk. David and I decided to have lunch together every day. Mark and I made a pact that we'd see each other after school.

A lot had happened to me since September, and I wasn't sure how everything was going to work out. But I was sure of one thing. Now I had three good friends. And that meant a lot.

I was looking forward to what would happen next. I guess that meant that I agreed with Dad. This *had* been the right move, after all.

ABOUT THE AUTHOR

CYNTHIA STOWE was born in New Britain, Connecticut, and now lives in western Massachusetts with her husband, Robert. She has worked with kids for many years, both as a school psychologist and as a teacher.

In this story, she wanted to write a funny book that looks at a difficult subject: moving. "When we laugh," she says, "we can often gain understanding about things that make us cry. I hope that *Home Sweet Home, Good-bye* brings some laughter and understanding into our world."